Tales From
Merlin's Pal

Best wishes
Richard Small

Richard Small

Edward Gaskell
Devon

Edward Gaskell publishers
Riverbank Cottages
Bideford
Devon
EX39 4AS

ISBN 978-1-906769-83-3

Tales From Merlin's Pal

Richard Small

Typeset, printed and bound by
Lazarus Press
6 Grenville Street
Bideford
Devon
EX39 3DX
www.lazaruspress.com

This book of short stories in all their forms is dedicated to those who neither hide from, nor fear, the truth and who can appreciate an alternative view on life.

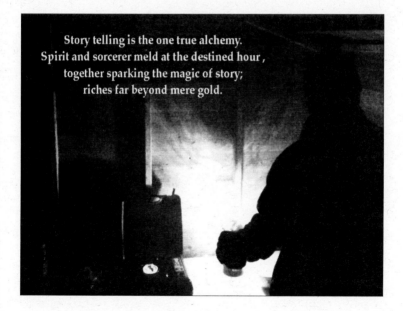

Story telling is the one true alchemy.
Spirit and sorcerer meld at the destined hour,
together sparking the magic of story;
riches far beyond mere gold.

Edward Gaskell
publishers
DEVON

'There is a moment in time and space, where the world of opposites resides in fleeting but perfect harmony. The unknown beckons from beyond that gateway. Having crossed the threshold you will never be the same again.'

'Nothing in this universe can exist without an opposite. No sadness, no joy; No fear, no courage; No darkness, no light; No death, no life.'

'Despite your own belief of normality, somewhere beyond the gateway is an undeniable difference that awaits your arrival, for, know this, we are only here, we only exist, because somewhere out in the beyond, there is an opposite.'

'You are, only because, *it is.'*

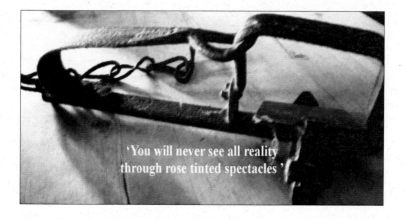

'You will never see all reality through rose tinted spectacles '

Front Cover

Merlin was a golden retriever, a real character, he belonged to my then wife but I often enjoyed his company, which I shared to his last breath. He's here *now*, because he *was*. A happy go lucky creature never short of food or admirers – how fortunate is that in life?

Richard Small

About the author

Richard is just a plain bloke who did his best in life, sometimes enthusiastic, sometimes lazy, sometimes clever and sometimes dopey. You'll know him quite well by the time you've read a couple of his stories. He wrote them for you. Nothing would vindicate his efforts more than for these tales to be read and shared with others. It is not so much to ask, is it?

Contents

1

Well met, on a bridge to the other side.

A fading summer Sun had hushed the land to sleep. High up on the old bridge that spanned the tributary, a clumsily dressed, thin young man in his early thirties stood wide awake in the stillness. Transfixed like a rabbit caught in headlights, captivated by the swirling torrent far below - a torrent that rushed on unquestioningly in its blind search for the ocean's dark but welcoming shroud. By two in the morning all was graveyard silent and he was still there lost in thought, the air was warm and his frayed T shirt and old trousers were all he needed that night, or any night. . . his body and soul braced forlorn on the wrong side of the railings.

Suddenly a voice shattered the silence and with it went any peace he might have had. The young man nearly jumped out of his skin, for he'd not seen or heard a soul for three hours or more. 'Steady on mate,' said the voice. 'I didn't mean to make you jump.' The young man gripped the railings even more tightly with both hands, pulling his back firm against the bars, his mind now in turmoil, for he'd hoped to end it all alone.

There was something of an Aussie twang to the voice from the dark; its owner came closer, stopped a few feet away, rested his folded arms on the parapet and continued talking as though finding a walker, never mind an erstwhile jumper, on the bridge at this God forsaken hour was quite a normal occurrence.

'So, what you doing here then, young fellah? Sure is a lovely night and what a beautiful view you've got yourself here.

Betcha that river's full of life down there, them crabs and fishes don't sleep at night yer know.'

The young man didn't know what to say, in fact he didn't want to say anything; he just wanted this bloke to clear off to whence he came. He'd been content with his prior misery. However, curiosity had the better of him and he sensed a non judgemental calm from his surprise visitor, 'Crumbs, you made me jump, no pun intended, what on earth are you doing here at this hour?'

'Well young fellah, I could ask you the same, but me, I'm what you might call of no fixed abode, a gentleman of the road, homeless if you like. It's not so bad you understand, though it was before; loads of things went wrong before, lost the missus and kids, parents died, injured at work. . . in the army I was you know. Oh they paid me off all right but pound notes were no compensation nor cure for my ills back then.'

'So what *does* brings you to this road, this bridge, tonight then?' the apprentice jumper asked again.

'Oh, dunno really, just going with feelings, always follow the good feelings I say. When you walk with a smile on your face you'll always get some coming back your way. It just felt right to go further south, more rural, nicer people; chance of a few jobs on a farm or something. Food in the hedgerows, berries and the like – yeah, that's about it really – just feelings and as it was a warm night I thought I'd take advantage of the cooler air and quiet road. Then I met you, nature-watching from your fine perch on my bridge.'

'Sorry about that,' said the reticent jumper, who somehow felt empathy for the ex-soldier and his losses in life. He realised that somewhere, way back, we're all linked together somehow. In fact, this happy tramp had suffered far more than he ever had himself. 'You never thought of ending it all then?' he enquired.

'Yeah mate, I *thought* about it but when I got here some young fellah had nicked my spot. You gonna be long?' The jovial tramp's smile could just be made out in the moonlight.

For some peculiar reason, perhaps contagion, it appeared amusing to the would-be jumper and he smiled back, 'Oh yeah, good one, very droll,' he said. The strange thing was, the thoughts that drove his racked body to the bridge were changing and as the thoughts changed so did his feelings. In fact, the tramp was right, it was a beautiful view, it was a great night, the moon smiled down on a land at peace with itself and he, for that moment felt part of that. What had possessed him to ever want to throw such beauty away?

'I'm coming back over,' said the reformed jumper.

'No mate, stay there, you'll be fine, in fact, I'll join you over there – that little bit of fear, the adrenalin rush just spices life up a bit at times, makes you feel more alive than ever – come on, shift over a bit, give us a hand.'

The pair of them nattered away for what seemed like hours, like two long lost pals reunited.

Interspersed with tales from down under, of joy and woes, the gentleman of the road implanted his wisdom and set the seeds of hope and resolution in his young friend's mind; he'd given him a gentle push – in the right direction. Good thoughts began to bring the young man good feelings and they filled his very soul and body.

'Well, I reckon I'll thank you kindly for all your help and wisdom and be on my way home now, for tomorrow I have much to begin.' So saying, the young man clambered roadside of the railings, his body and spirit lightened from the burdens he'd earlier carried to the bridge. Now it was as though he'd dropped them into the swirling depths below to be lost forever. He was now free and felt it, like somehow he'd paid off some long outstanding debt at last.

'So long mate, I'm gonna stay a while longer, before I make my way to the other side. You be good, you think happy, feel happy, and don't waste yer life. . . live it well.'

As the young, now rehabilitated, jumper reached the end of the bridge he suddenly realised he didn't even know this saviour's name, he turned and started to shout his question but there was no point in finishing the sentence, the kindly stranger had already gone. 'Oh well,' he thought, 'After his good deed tonight I hope at last he finds somewhere to rest in peace, he's obviously decided not to wait any longer on the bridge after all.'

That young man went home, made a better life, repaid that good deed a thousand times over and never forgot his friend the tramp, well met on the bridge to the other side. He resolved to share his story with anyone who would listen, just like he had listened that fateful night so many years ago.

And now you have heard it. I must leave you now, for there are others waiting in the darkness, on bridges they built for themselves.

If you would only look, you will find joy on every path. No matter how dark it seems.

**

'After the long slumber of ignorance, a single word can change a man forever.'

Nan Guo Zi

**

2

Fay, the homeless

Gathered in friendship, warm and comfortable at the window table of Maxime's café, the small group of ladies had eyes for the fine patisseries and ears for the inane tittle tattle gossip of the middle classes. They neither saw nor heard Fay's frail body sheltering from the rain, huddled against the low window of the grand entrance. Fay sought refuge there night and day but few ever sensed her presence and even fewer cared. They walked on by, mindlessly on their mobile phones, never aware of her cry for help. Despite her grubby and tattered clothes she was a pretty young woman of Chinese descent and had at one time been employed as a dish washer at Maxime's. Life had taken an irrevocable turn for the worse since the accident. Her home was now occupied by others, her job taken by a stranger and she had no one to talk to, no one to share her troubles and no shoulder to cry on. Try as she might, she could find no one who would listen, and try, she had. Fay had long stopped feeling the cold and damp of the English weather; somehow it didn't affect her anymore like it did those hurrying by with warm scarf and long coat.

The boisterous conversation in the café lurched from, 'of course our mortgage is paid off,' to 'hubby's new job' and 'the boss has his own yacht,' to 'how well the children are doing at university,' and 'of course Rupert wants to be a doctor,' well 'Daniel, our new under-gardener is so attractive and insists on bringing fresh flowers to the house for me every day.' 'We might move soon... there are some awful working-class people buying a house in the village.' 'Our cousin Matilda has a new book published you know... 'I don't think I should eat any more cake... perhaps I'll just have a special coffee to round it off.' 'Cointreau coffee here please, waiter.'

The indiscernible Fay could both hear and see it all but it made no difference, she could never be one of them. It seemed her lot to endure the desolation of unremitting hopelessness: alone, homeless, and unseen by the passing wealthy and poor alike.

The waiter keenly approached the ladies group, rubbing his hands with anticipation of a good tip. 'Where's my coffee?' asked the cake-filled lady who incidentally kept her posh hat on even indoors, 'Harrods you know... and not in a sale either!' Grovelling and ingratiating himself to the group, the waiter feigned a sincere apology and explained that they were short staffed due to the accident outside the café the other week. 'Hit and run driver, probably drunk, in a new BMW had run over and killed the Chinese girl who used to wash up. Not to worry, we've a new one but she's still learning. All will be back to normal soon. I'll fetch your coffee, ma'am.'

Outside in the mizzling rain, Fay's ghost would indeed be forever homeless and like so many others in shop doorways, simply invisible to any kindness, any justice.

**

*'The way you wake up is
the way you live your life.'*

**

3

A Mountain to Climb.

Compelled by worsening weather, he rested a while on his climb. He reached out with a trembling hand to a wall of stone to check his balance, his ankles twisting as they adjusted to the slope. Quietly, almost impossibly, he gasped for breath. It was as though the air he breathed had thinned; his muscles ached and his joints pained him like never before. But he must climb on, he cannot stop here, he must continue. Easing the pressure on his old shoulders from the thin straps of a worn canvas rucksack he began once more up the slope, the deep snow under his thin leather boots, now crisp

with frost. A bitingly cold wind blew over the ridge from the east. It would have almost been a blessing if his hands were numb with cold but all he felt was a relentlessly fierce pain through his woefully inadequate woollen gloves. The unseasonably bad weather had taken him somewhat by surprise, as too had his own age and ability to make a climb so easily done in his youth. He'd been a good climber once, a keen sportsman, always striving to succeed and lift the trophy, even if only for a photo at the finish. Now, was a struggle of epic proportions, the trophy at the end of this climb was life itself, to fail was death. He was alone - this was not the place for thrill seekers, for even they were safe at home. Every agonising step was an enormous struggle, each one was short and laboured, the wind tugged at his clothes trying to confound him but he was solemnly resolute, it was only he that could save himself.

He stopped again, gathered his remaining strength and then plodded on inexorably, miserably, even tearfully, his stooped body leaning into the hill before him. This was no glorious race, with the eyes of the world watching with bated breath, this was a lonely private struggle for which he only had himself to blame, the only eyes that watched were those of Angels, wringing their helpless hands in pity and sorrow.

He was no stranger to this place, he was just a stranger to the circumstances, in a self reflective moment he remembered how strong he was in his youth. Recalling those youthful days had helped him a little, bolstered his spirits and squinting past his frosted eyelashes he could just make out the summit. It wasn't so far now. Not in distance perhaps but in time it seemed like a million miles. Darkness would soon be on him and drag him down like a pack of black Hyenas, if he falls he may not be able to rise again, he must not fail - it is not yet his time. His tired muscles, weak with age and cramped with burned out effort hardly responded to his desperate call.

Finally, only moments to spare with the fast closing shadow of the grim reaper behind him on the slope, he arrived. He kicked off the snow from his boots, shut the door behind him and shuffled through to a warm kitchen and the kettle. He placed his rucksack on the table and picked something out for tea.

Pensioner and widower, 87 year old Edmund Scott, was home from the shops.

Story inspired by watching an elderly gentleman in the street expending all his effort merely to make his way home. You too must have seen these warriors of age in their daily battles. Give them a thought. April 2016 Devon

**

*'It is not because things are difficult that we do not dare.
It is because we do not dare that they are difficult.'*

**

4

Hope: does it live on, or die in despair?

She lived on the sixth floor of a block of 1960s flats, one of the few drab grey monoliths still standing in the area; a fitting memorial to a long-gone and failed social experiment. It was one of those places where you could live for several years and never even see a neighbour let alone talk to one.

The living room, still with its 1960s wallpaper of nondescript green leaf did not fail to show its age. The room gave access to a tiny balcony via the windows that faced south and enjoyed far reaching views beyond the conurbation to gently rolling farm clad hills and some still surviving ancient woodland. It was a bright and sunny day and with reasonable eyesight one  could see, soaring majestically, a lone Buzzard harried by rooks high above the woods. The Buzzard always seemed to be able to rise above the conflict and merely dipped his wings and changed direction to avoid the attack, moving on in unperturbed serenity, borne aloft by nature's generous gifts.

'Hey, come quick and see the birds,' called her friend Solomon excitedly as he watched the buzzard through the open window, 'Wow! Now that really is beautiful, don't miss it, come on!'

Solomon had been a good friend for many years and, when allowed, an occasional visitor who had always sought to brighten her life. He seemed an ever hopeful, ever positive warrior in his late thirties, whilst she was an ever negative worrier in her early forties.

'No, can't at the moment, there's a charity advert about children in need. . . poor things they don't stand a chance. . . anyway, East enders Omnibus is on next and I want to watch it again, they kill off one of the heroes next episode. . . I wonder who it will be. . . and you know I can't put the TV in the sunny room as I can't see the picture properly,' she moaned from her half bedroom half living room on the North side of the flat; in general mostly cold and often damp around the single glazed window that over looked the backs of shops and a derelict factory unit; black mildew lived undisturbed and contentedly behind her mother's old wardrobe.

'I know,' replied Solomon brightly, 'let's go out for a walk to the park and feed the ducks, see the squirrels or something. It'll be fun, come on.'

There was a considerable pause before her reply, as the advert wasn't quite finished, 'No, I don't want to, it will be dark soon and I'm not paying good money for bread just to throw it away on some old ducks that should be able to care for themselves.'

Solomon's exploring eyes were drawn to some children far below, boys and girls, playing football on the little council green between the car parks; it looked like great fun, he could sense their laughter and high spirits. 'There are some children playing on the green, let's go and watch and perhaps be able to join in if we're lucky.'

There was another long pause as he heard the theme tune to her programme finishing, 'Certainly not, horrid kids, their parents should keep them indoors. I bet it's them doing all that graffiti too.'

'Okay,' sighed the ever hopeful Solomon, now coming more to the real purpose of this visit. He brightened his voice again and, while reaching into his jacket pocket to reassuringly touch his as yet undelivered bundle of love letters, continued, 'I have an idea, let me take you out for a meal, and then we'll go to the cinema. I hear there's a great film on at the new Multi-screen, all about a young woman who finally meets the man of her dreams but then struggles to find a way to tell him, it's supposed to be very funny. What do you say?'

'No, I'm not interested in a daft film about some stupid woman chasing an even more stupid bloke. It doesn't appeal to me at all. I've got some dinner in the fridge anyway; you go out to eat if you like. . . I don't think there's enough for two as it is. . . it's a mix of various things that I've had leftover during the week. It's all go this cooking lark, all go I tell you. I'm a slave to my kitchen, always stuck in, that's me.'

Always keen to please her, 'How about I get a Chinese take away, freshly cooked, very tasty, that would be nice, my treat, and I'll fetch it too,' offered Solomon, his friendly voice again reaching out to her.

'No, don't like Chinese food, never liked it since I overheard someone in a post office queue. . . and what a damn long one it was too. . . they should have more counter staff I say . . . . anyway they said that they knew of a neighbour's friend who knew someone who'd holidayed in Krastanovika where they'd eaten a Chinese meal and it made them all ill.'

'Now there's an idea', said Solomon with far-off dreaming eyes gazing to the right and, along with his soul, drawn towards the setting Sun; a beautiful sky that glowed yellow through orange to the prettiest red that he'd ever seen; 'Why don't we go on a nice holiday together, it would do you good to get out and I've not had a holiday for years now, what with the pressure of my charity work on top of full time hospital duties. Yes, that would be wonderful. What do you say? What about a cruise? I'll help with money if that's a problem.'

'No, I'd be sea sick for a start, never was any good at travelling, I haven't really done any since I remember my mum saying I was sick on a bus when I was two or three. No, you go if you like; I have every thing I need here.'

The theme tune played itself out to the bitter end and she slowly got up and pushed her feet into some tatty and cheap slippers and stubbed out her cigarette before it went too far down the filter. Pulling an old dark cardigan tighter around her shoulders she walked through to the sunny living room. Very unlike him, Solomon had already gone. She half wondered, half hoped that he may have gone to fetch that takeaway, she was quite hungry now and that rubbish in the fridge was really destined for a bin of the same name. As the sunshine began to disappear she pulled closed the window and drew the curtains against the setting Sun and impending cold of evening; she flicked the switch on her coal effect electric fire and she waited for the phone or the doorbell to ring. Solomon was truly such a fine chap, such good company; she missed him now he was gone and she sat waiting hopefully for his return. The doorbell rang and she quickly rose to her feet, she'd been thinking about the cinema again and the holiday too, how great it would be to share Solomon's wisdom and happy company on such an adventure of a lifetime. Quickly she tidied the cushions and excitedly walked to the door, a spring in her step, pausing only to adjust her clothes and hair in the mirror. She opened the door with a bright smile that soon disappeared when she saw two uniformed constables standing in the dim light of the concrete hallway. They could see she was shocked and the first said calmly, 'May we come in Ma'am; we have some questions we'd like to ask you. Best you take a seat first.'

She sat down, perched on the edge of her two seat settee and clutching at her cardigan with both hands, 'Oh, dear, oh, dear, what is it, why are you here? she begged.

The first began again in a compassionate but official manner, 'It's about a gentleman by the name of Solomon Ma'am, we have some bad news, I'm afraid that there's no easy way Ma'am, it looks very much like suicide, if it's any consolation ma'am it would have been over very quickly, he couldn't have suffered at all.'

Shocked and totally surprised by such news as she could never have expected, she wondered why the officers knew to come to her door. 'But how did you know. . . ?'

The second officer completed her sentence for her, 'How did we know to come here? Well, the location of the body below those windows Ma'am and we also found a bundle of undelivered letters in his inner coat pocket with your name and address, that's how we found you so quickly. I know this is difficult Ma'am but we have to ask. Do you know any reason at all that could help with enquiries as to why he would jump to his death? Anything at all ma'am that could help us close the case.'

Her hands wrung at her cardigan, dear Solomon, gone. . . 'Oh, no, officer, none at all. Why, he was the most kindly, gentle soul, so full of life, full of hopes and dreams, always happy, positive, he loved nature, travel, good food. . . he loved life itself. . . in fact I never knew anyone with so much to live for. I'm so sorry I cannot help you more, that's really all I ever knew of him. . . poor lovely Solomon.'

'Thank you for your patience Ma'am, we'll let ourselves out, sorry about the bad news Ma'am.'

As they stood in the doorway before closing the door, the second officer spoke kindly, 'We can't let you have the letters yet Ma'am, must go to the coroner first. When that's all over I'm sure they will be forwarded to you, I'm sure that's what he would have wanted all the time.' The door closed quietly but firmly on one sad lady, in the background the theme tune began for Coronation Street; she sat motionless, lost in thought, clutching at her cardigan.

Following her great loss, as the weeks slipped by she began to change her habits. Sometimes she would watch the children play their games outside the flats, occasionally thinking that Solomon was there playing with them. . . oh, the laughter, such happy times. She would buy a Chinese meal to eat at home, pausing to savour some delicacy and consider how there was always enough for two. She moved her two seat settee around to face the south window and often looked across the fields to the buzzards soaring spectre like over the ancient woods. She bought some bright new clothes of her own and stopped smoking. Finally when Solomon's letters were released by the coroner's court, she would sit at the window and read them over again, often smiling at his kind words, often missing his compassionate and uplifting company. Sometimes she thought he still visited, heard his footsteps, heard his laughter, 'Silly, silly me,' she thought.

Meanwhile sitting, as unnoticed as ever he was, on the cushions close by her side, Solomon watched contented, at last he'd made her happy, it was all he'd ever hoped for.

**

Nietzsche, the German philosopher once said,
'Hope is the greatest of all evils,
for it prolongs the torment of man.'
Now *you* decide.

61

**

The Pharaoh's heart (conscience) was weighed against a feather to see if he was good enough to pass to the afterlife. In the following story, what you read is a measure of your interest, what you think is a measure of your soul. The innate in you will always know the truth.

5

Harry's Rescue

Dave's feelings were more than a little hurt as he recalled his wife Beth wagging a finger at him from the kitchen doorway at home saying, and not without a touch of inherited venom in her voice, 'If you *don't* go to mother's seventieth, I *will* - and I *won't* be coming back!' He knew she meant it too; she'd been the love of his life but was quite difficult to live with now, for sure. However, he didn't want to lose his home and family and so it was that one autumn Friday afternoon they arrived at the cosy but fateful hotel on the south coast. The family had clubbed together in a haphazardly unequal way to pay for the special event. Dave suspected that his share was considerably more than his brother-in-law Nathan's. Nathan, an astute and manipulative man, was almost as mean as his mother and had been named after a frequently friendly local butcher.

Beth and Dave enjoyed a reasonably friendly evening on their own, as they had travelled down a day earlier than the rest of the party. Their room was pleasant and comfortable but without a sea view, as those rooms were reserved for Beth's mother and company. As they settled into the plush bed and put out the lights, Beth warned Dave once more of the consequences of alienating her mother, 'Don't you dare be rude and don't you dare wander off and leave the party. We're only here to give mum a good time for her special birthday.' Both room and mood plunged into an even deeper darkness. Dave mumbled his agreement and turned over with some sadness. He couldn't stand the mother-in-law, he could hardly choke the words out to even speak to her, he certainly never called her 'mum' or even by her first name. He called her Mrs Briarley on the odd occasion he was obliged to converse. Dave was fully aware that his mother-in-law was of the opinion that he was a useless, weird and unpleasant object that would have been better off being put down at birth. She hadn't attended their wedding, had written Dave specifically out of her will and refused to acknowledge Dave and Beth's three now grown up children. None of that bothered Dave as he doubted she had any money to leave and her absence from his life was a blessed and possibly divine intervention – to his way of thinking anyway.

In general, Dave interacted well with most people, he liked chatting to the landlady at breakfast, he enjoyed greeting people in the street and always had sound advice for his children on the odd occasion they might distain to listen. Beth had few friends but wasn't too bothered, they were mostly idiots out there anyway, and especially the man she regretted ever marrying.

The family, various attached partners and their children arrived midday and after a brief exchange of obligatory greetings, went to their rooms to rest. At least that's what they said they were doing.

Dave was at a loose end, he'd read all the hotel's newspapers, perused the paintings on the wall, mulled over the menus a few times and stared out of the window at the sea. And he knew worse was to come! He returned to his hotel room where he found Beth sitting on the bed, filing her nails over his pillow and preparing for the party. 'For God's sake, stop moping about, why don't you do something useful for a change!' she exclaimed, having been quite happy with her own company.

'I think I'll go out for a walk along the beach,' Dave said almost as though asking permission. He suffered a little from a self esteem issue.

'Right, that's it, all my family here and you want to go for a walk on the beach, that's charming isn't it?' she retorted, 'Well go then and be back well before the dinner, you be back by four, or else.'

Dave wondered as he turned the door handle what the 'or else' might be, but was left in no doubt when Beth assured him, 'If you're not back for mum's party then you'll be dying a lonely old man!'

As Dave wandered left along the beach and away from the hotel and edge of town, those words played on his mind, in fact he would never forget them to his dying day. He just couldn't understand how someone could even think such things, he didn't want to be lonely at all, let alone die in that way.

The further Dave walked from town the more he began to relax, the sea air, the autumn sunshine, gulls calling him to look at how well they flew, small sandstone cliffs and a sailing boat far out at sea. . . all compounded to make life so much better, so much happier. Dave checked his watch, plenty of time, he could go another half hour at least before turning back. Just up in front and round a small promontory, he spotted what looked like 1940s war time defences. 'Worth a look, this,' Dave thought, 'this is interesting.' It seemed like there may also have been a small landing pier at some time, though the sea had brought the once proud and staunch metal framework in a tangle to its knees. There was a recent chain link fence with a sign attached, **'MoD Property. NO ENTRY. DANGER.**

However there was an easy gap in the fence near the cliff face and it looked like people had made a habit of passing through, 'Perhaps fishermen,' thought Dave as he stood unashamed and excited on forbidden ground. 'This is more like it,' Dave chuckled to himself, 'knocks the socks off sitting down to dinner with the mother-in-law.'

Back at the hotel the family was beginning to assemble in the lounge. Pretentious greetings intermingled with handfuls of free nuts and canapé's.

'Like a flock of vultures they are dear,' confided the landlady's husband. He was sharply rebuked, 'Shhh if they hear you say something like that, they could easily write us bad reviews, they seem that sort. You be on your best behaviour and take 'em some more nuts out. . . I'm helping the cook now with the meal preparations.' 'Oh, and the nice chap who came last night with his wife has gone for a walk along the sea front, said he'd be back before four, keep an eye out for him, poor man.'

By now, a new self empowered Dave had drifted off into childhood dreams and memories and was exploring the remains of reinforced concrete and twisted metal, all of which were unsighted from the town. . . 'and for good reason no doubt,' thought Dave.

The green sea algae had made Dave's new playground more slippery than ice. Disaster was inevitable and not slow in arriving.

'You stupid, stupid man,' his self admonition a mixture of grief and annoyance. . . instead of looking where he was going he'd glanced at his watch. . . he'd fell, twisting his ankle into the bargain. 'Idiot, idiot, idiot,' he said with more than a wince of pain, looking at his only good clothes covered in sand.

'Oh well, nothing for it but brush myself down and limp straight back to face the music I suppose,' but his foot had slipped between the rusty metal lattice and he couldn't pull it back. The more Dave panicked the worse it became, the injury was already beginning to swell his ankle and making extrication nigh on impossible. What was he to do? He was more in fear of his domineering wife's retribution than the more imminent disaster of drowning, a fate incidentally, which did not cross his mind for some minutes. Drowning? Dave looked about him, the tide was out, yes, but it would be coming back. Even if he could sit up he was still below the seaweed that had made its home on the old pier stanchions. . . if he didn't get out he would drown, he was trapped and going to drown. . . slowly and inexorably. Dave panicked even more and began to shout, even scream, for help. He paused to listen hopefully for a reply, surely there must be others out here, fishermen, dog walkers and the like. . . the only sound that came back to his eager ears was the distant soft swoosh of gentle waves on sand and the hungry cry of a seagull looking for something dead or dying on the beach. He checked his pockets. . . his wallet, car keys, a creased up hotel menu and his mobile phone! 'Thank you God, thank you,' beamed a relieved Dave. His fingers fumbled to turn it on, it seemed to be working and there was still life in the battery. He decided to contact the hotel, he really must speak to his wife first. . . she would understand. Then he'd call the emergency services, the coastguard would be best, perhaps the fire-brigade too, and why not an ambulance because that ankle didn't look too good, possibly broken, certainly ligaments gone. Dave used the number on the hotel menu to dial, he had to try twice as his fingers were shaking so much. . . he put the receiver to his ears and waited. . . nothing. He looked at the phone screen, 'no signal'. Dave could have wept, no blasted signal, the one time in his life when he really needed the phone and there was no signal! He tied again and again, trying different positions, holding the phone high, holding it next to the steel work. . . none of it made any difference. Dave tried to sit up so that he could reach his ankle but the angle his foot was pinned meant that his knee would not allow it. There was still plenty of time, the tide would surely take several hours, I mean it only comes in once a day doesn't it? Help would arrive from the hotel long before that. He called out loudly again.

Meanwhile the Briarley clan were gathering in the lounge in preparation for their celebratory dining experience. The guest of honour, a paradoxical accolade, circulated importantly and in her time honoured fashion badmouthed the rest of the population, particularly her dear daughter's repugnant wastrel husband, who she was quite pleased to note was missing. . . 'With a bit of luck run over somewhere,' she thought with no smile.

A young and pleasant waitress appeared at the dining room door, 'If you would like, you can all be seated and we can serve you drinks at the table. Please come though when you are ready.' Slowly the family wandered in to the dining room and looked for their name cards, strategically planned so that Mrs Briarley's favourites sat opposite and next to her, with those she openly detested to the far edges of her vision. It wasn't long before Dave's absence was noticed due to the empty chair at the door end of the table. Mrs Briarley took this as an intended personal insult, my goodness she'd like to see him suffer, her hands twitched as if gripping him by his throat. 'Where is he then Beth, drunk, lost, asleep? Or have you come to your senses and left him at last. It's what I would have done a long time ago.' Some of the clan mumbled their conditioned approval, while others, fiddling with their napkins, kept an embarrassed silence, not wishing to be embroiled in the usual vitriol before having what they hoped would be a pleasant and digestible dinner.

Far away, along the beach and out of sight, Dave's mood swung wildly, from exhausted, resigned peace, tinged with hope of imminent rescue, (perhaps the phone had worked after all - it could be being traced and located as he lay there), to a sobbing helpless despair and desperation. The thought crossed his mind that a nearby broken bottle was almost within reach; one good effort and it would be in his hands, along with his own destiny. When the tide was closing in and no sign of rescue in sight he could cut off his foot at the ankle – or failing that – finish his life quickly with the broken glass to his throat.

Just as Dave was choosing his own dreadful destiny on the remote and deserted beach, so the Briarley family were choosing their favourite starters in the warm Georgian dining room of Hotel Astraea.

Dave's voice was beginning to fail and the adrenalin wear off, he shivered without noticing and his mind wandered into a day dream, to a place where he felt no pain. He was startled awake by a voice from somewhere behind him, a man's voice, calm, strong and confident, 'Hello, old chap, you seem to be in a bit of bother. Perhaps I can help.' And, as he moved closer into Dave's sight, 'my name's Harry, I'm from around here, spend a great deal of time at this old Royal Engineers pier myself you know, fascinating place.'

Dave thought of the worn path by the hole in the fence and put two and two together. 'Strewth, you made me jump Harry, so good to see another soul down here, I feared I was alone. I slipped and my ankle's stuck in the lattice work, it'll need cutting free I think.'

Harry carefully inspected the trapped ankle with an almost clinical interest, as though he was no stranger to such things, and then sat down close by Dave on a fallen steel girder. He spoke comfortingly with calmness and authority, 'you're not wrong there Dave, the authorities will have to bring some equipment to cut the steel. Meanwhile, try and relax the best you can, there's nothing more you can do about it. I'll stay with you all the way, so don't you worry about a thing.' Looking straight into Dave's half closed eyes, Harry lent forward, elbows on knees and concluded, 'You won't be the first that's done this . . . and I somehow doubt you'll be the last.' He smiled a little and gave a short reassuring laugh but none the less, Dave sensed an overwhelming empathy coming from Harry. Dave felt a warm sense of comfort flow over him, washing away all his fears, thank God he was saved. Harry's kind and somehow authoritative voice put him at ease, at peace. Dave looked at his rescuer with more than a hint of hero worship. Harry was a little shorter and younger than Dave but was powerfully built. Dave wouldn't be surprised if Harry was in the military in some capacity. Certainly, despite the horror of the situation Harry was taking it all in his stride, like he'd been there, seen that and done that all before. Dave felt blessed indeed that Harry had turned up, it was obvious now that the situation would be re-solved satisfactorily and naturally. Back at the Hotel there were blessings too. . . mostly for the size of the main course portions. The waitress noted that Dave's chair was still empty, 'Are we still waiting for someone? Shall I keep some of the servings back in case they turn up late?' She asked with a smile.

Beth started to speak but was beaten to it by her mother, 'No, you can clear away the place setting, he won't be joining us. We're here to have a good time, not worry about some waster with no manners.' One of his nieces, a kindly girl of good dis-position towards him tried Dave's mobile number, perhaps she could send a covert warning of what was happening at the hotel, but only the messaging service kicked in, Dave was not answering wherever he was. They returned to the jolly matter of fine food and plenty of it, 'Good job Dave paid his share up front Beth dear,' confided her mother with a knowing, some might say patronizing look, 'You've wasted half your life on him, whatever was wrong with that nice boy you went out with before, whatever his name was?'

'I told him to be back mother, he's so uncaring and selfish, I hope it doesn't spoil your party,' Beth replied, already making private, vengeful plans for Dave's unhappy future. She would see he suffered as long as he lived for this embarrassment.

Harry looked across at Dave and smiled kindly, 'Don't worry Dave, all will be well in the end, you'll see, just have courage. Far beyond his ability to understand why, Dave watched calmly as short, soft waves began to wash over Harry's feet. Dave was given comfort and strength by Harry's stoic resolution in the face of danger, that and the fact Dave had already exhausted himself with his earlier exertions. The onset of hypothermia was dulling some of his senses and the sea water that began gently lapping over his own feet seemed warm and agreeable, even welcoming.

At the hotel, puddings were being served to already stuffed stomachs, most of which were looking forward to a lie down on their beds for the afternoon. Beth was amazed at how much her mother could pack away, 'She was certainly a special woman, one to be admired,' Beth thought quietly.

'Hey! There's still money in the kitty. . . special coffees all round eh waitress,' shouted Nathan as small bits of fudge cake decorated the tablecloth in front of him - A grand end to a party.

At the beach, Dave thought of the party that he'd missed. He'd always been grateful for a good dinner and he was sorry he'd failed his wife and children by not being there for them. He imagined what Beth's mother would be saying about him . . . then he dismissed such negative thoughts. They just didn't seem appropriate for the moment and they certainly wouldn't help the situation. Warming soft waves gently lifted then covered more of his body now. Harry still sat on the nearby girder, water up to his waist but remaining resolute, still strong and with a compassionate yet empowering smile.

Dave was to feel no more pain from his trapped ankle and with his earlier plan for the broken glass long forgotten, he fell peacefully into his final sleep under the gently rising water.

Postscript

After being alerted by the landlady of 'Hotel Astraea', the authorities found and recovered Dave's body. It was the second time they had been to the old MoD site that year. Harry was quite right in what he'd said and they had to use cutting equipment to free Dave's leg too.

Beth left the car and all Dave's belongings at the hotel and travelled home with one of her children and her mother. They excitedly discussed divorce plans all the way. It was only when, a week later, a police officer called that Beth found out Dave's lifeless body had been found on the beach. 'Don't distress yourself too much - he wouldn't have known anything about it,' they said. 'It would have been over very quickly, and he wouldn't have suffered.'

Beth's mother smiled, now at last she could move in with her daughter and be looked after properly.

Dave sat with Harry beyond the fence on forbidden ground, they sat together on the girder chatting happily about old times when life was good and they watched with curiosity as twice each day the sea would cover them like a blanket, like the gods covering a sleeping child from the cold.

At last, Harry was no longer alone. Perhaps one day someone else will join their party because they will always be there, waiting.

**

'He who dies while he lives shall not die when he dies.'

**

'It is required of every man,' the ghost returned,
'that the spirit within him should walk abroad among his fellow-men, and travel far and wide; and, if that spirit goes not forth in life, it is condemned to do so after death.'

Charles Dickens

**

6

Life On The Moors

As in life, a story can have various endings, each of them created by choices made in the mind of the reader. In this story you will inevitably come across choices with which you may or may not agree. Such is the way of life.

This is the thought provoking tale of a late 18th century peasant family as they struggle across desolate moor-land seeking a better life on the other side, a place free from betrayal and starvation. Will they find it? Will they make the right choices? Would you?

The date is 1786 and like many peasants of the day, George Dinnicombe was another hard-working victim of the social system, often surviving on subsistence wages in return for giving his all, his life, his family, and his soul. He was hungry, not just for decent food but for the opportunity to provide well for his family. George himself was born to pauper parents in the winter of 1752 and when old enough to work was given away and bound to a Thomas Reid, owner of a black-smiths and farrier business not far from the pretty North Devon village of Loxhore.

George did well as apprentice to Thomas Reid, a kindly and likeable gentleman with an excellent reputation for horses and ironwork. George proved himself over and over again as a willing worker and a keen learner and soon became indispensable to Reid's family business. Life was as good as could be expected for a working class man.

Back in the spring of 1774, then twenty two, George married a God fearing and kind-hearted young lass from Stoke Rivers, Phoebe Goulde. Phoebe was the same age as George and also from an impoverished family; her father had died of Smallpox the year before she married. George and Phoebe were to be blessed with three strong and healthy children, William 11, Thomas 9, and their sister Sarah 6.

Old Mr Reid, the owner of the business had two grown sons, Mark and his younger rival sibling Luke, of whom it must be said was a downright wastrel and a most disappointing son for the fair-minded and kindly Thomas Reid. It was a bad day for all when Thomas Reid was finally laid to rest. Thomas' funeral was a fine affair and well attended by the local community, in particular the many that were in his debt for past favours. None were surprised by the absence of the spendthrift Luke, who had ridden into Barnstaple town to celebrate his inheritance in the only way he knew. Subsequently his drinking and gambling incurred debts upon the business and despite his brother Mark's best efforts they soon had to let workers go and evict loyal and trusty servants of many years.

On the third of March 1786 it was George's turn and he was the last to go. The business had failed completely by then, due to Luke's so called 'friends' calling in their markers.

Mark Reid retained a small cottage from the estate in which he continued to live with his grieving mother. None of these events were going to be easy for anyone. By the dying heat of the forge, the two men stood in solemnity already aware of the other's mind, 'I'm deeply sorry George. We've grown up together here and I had great hopes we would all grow old in dignity and peace together too. It's not to be. The cottage you live in is no longer mine. You will have to move out, I'm truly sorry. I can tell you how bad it is, the horses we have, those few that are left, I cannot even afford to feed. I'm not sure how I will survive but am hopeful one of my father's friends may have pity on me and find me a position.'

'I'm sorry too sir for your loss, don't you worry about us sir, I shall think of something. . . don't you worry sir. I shall go and speak with Phoebe and we'll make our plans,' said George with a confidence in his voice that belied his sense of total loss. Mark had been like a brother to him all these years and old Mr Reid had been like a kindly uncle all through his service. It wasn't the first time George had struggled alone and he didn't suppose it would be the last either. As he walked away from the smithy, across the once weed free, inner cobbled yard and under the barn to the lane outside, he met Luke coming the other way. As usual he was the worse for drink but treated George with the respect that bullies often have for those who are, in nature and in stature, their betters, 'Sorry to see you go George old chap, you're a fine fellow, fine wife too I'll say.'

Something in the back of his mind inspired George to ask a favour, 'Luke, sir, if you cannot feed the horses, could you see your way to let me have one in payment for all the times I saved you from troubles in the past?'

'George old chap, help yourself, no, tell you what, I'll pick one out myself and tether her outside the barn for you. That big bay with the black mane is a fine horse. You leave it with me. You can trust me not to let you down.' With that he staggered off to confront his poor brother over some trifling amount he still needed.

George walked thoughtfully to the comparative hovel they called a cottage but nevertheless a home of happy times, an emerging plan taking shape in his mind. At the back of the cottage was a run down open farm cart in need of some attention, what with that fine horse Luke had promised and a few running repairs to the cart they could use it to start a new life where there was more work. Many a traveller seeking the farrier at the smithy had shared their tales of riches and fine living in towns such as Bristol. Riches fostered by the ships that sailed to and from the new world. This was a bold but fine plan.

Phoebe listened quietly as he broke the news. She thought a while then said quietly, 'Why George dear, could they not tell you last week when you would have had a chance of work at the hiring fair. You are a good man with fine skills, you would have found work to be sure. . . and now it is three months to the next one. . . and us homeless with winter not yet past.' 'That Luke will surely go to hell, for certain he should, I pity his poor mother, God bless her.' The children, though not fully understanding the implications, had heard the news. They had such faith in their father, they were not afraid, it seemed like an adventure.

'We will leave tomorrow morning. While I prepare the cart you must gather what little we have to take. There may be a few root vegetables still good enough to lift. . . William, you can do that. Otherwise just help your mother in whatever she asks. While there is some daylight left I will begin on the old cart,' and with that he was gone to the rear of the cottage, tools in hand.

That night they all had a good supper and kept the fire banked well, no point in leaving firewood for the next tenant. Nobody slept well that night, all minds in turmoil over the unknown.

As a pale grey March dawn approached slowly from the east bringing with it a cold wind off the moors, George was already preparing to leave. He had on his working clothes and thick coat as his old boots clumped up the stony lane for one last time to the stables. He was in for a dreadful shock, no fine bay horse awaited him, just an old nag of twenty years or more. The poor animal was more suited to feeding the hounds at his Lordship's hunt than pull a cart.

George was staring at the old grey mare in a mixture of disbelief, sorrow and surprise, when Mark's voice startled him from the barn doorway. 'George, George, my dear friend, I am so sorry this has happened. Luke was angry I had no more money for him yesterday so he took all the horses, leaving only old Molly here. He said she probably wouldn't reach town alive anyway. It's all there is my friend, all there is and nothing anymore to be done about it.'

'Never you mind sir, not your doing, we'll care for her, make the best of it as we always have,' George assured, as he released the tether to walk Molly down to the cottage.

Mark held out his hand, George took it and the warmth of fellowship flowed in their veins. As Mark released his grip, George looked in his hand. . . a golden Guinea looked back. 'No need to say anything George, take it for any emergency you might face. It's all I have, I wish it were more, for you were ever a better brother to me than that wastrel drunkard. I wish you all well and tell you, I will never forget you and your loyal service to my father. Goodbye George.'

Outside their humble cottage, Phoebe looked in astonishment at the old horse but young Sarah instantly loved the quiet gentleness of the old grey. They'd never had a horse before.

'I know, I know,' agreed George, 'I know she's old but if we are careful and do our share of walking too, we'll survive. If we stay here we'll starve for sure. We must always make the best of what we have. Come on boys, you can help me harness her in the shafts.'

Their adventure to a new freedom had begun. Most roads in those days were very poor, almost impassable in places. It became fashionable for the rich to improve some important roads and charge people for using them. George chose instead to take isolated and remote moorland tracks for a number of reasons, it would be very many miles shorter, it avoided the levies of toll roads and there would be free grazing for the family's new horse.

It all began well, with the children and Sarah walking alongside, George leading the horse, encouraging with kind words gleaned from so many years of his trade. After a few miles they left the small tree filled valleys behind and started the steady climb on to the wilds of Exmoor. They stopped only briefly near mid day, for daylight was still valuable in the month of March. The pace was slow and dependant on Molly the horse, each hour would only see them another weary two miles along the ancient tracks.

Then, George smiled and looked back at his despondently trudging family, 'Look there, lady luck is smiling upon us.' He pointed to a small but well situated farmstead ahead and down to the right. It was only a gentle slope to the farm, it looked a touch run down but had all the essentials, running water, sheltered valley, small orchard, a wood for fuel and even a low lying pasture field that could be cultivated. Little Sarah wandered alongside and chatted to her new found childhood friend Molly the grey horse, who ambled slowly on at the perfect pace for the charming six year old. George waved an open hand to the farmer who was struggling with a broken fence. As they approached, they greeted each other warmly, one for the comfort of shelter and the other the comfort of company.

The farmer introduced himself as William Beer and as he did so, a pleasantly smiling plump lady wiping her hands on a cloth appeared at the open farm house door, 'and this is my good wife, Sarah.' And then, after hearing the traveller's story, William Beer insisted, 'You shall dine with us tonight and the barn is sound enough for shelter. . . it looks like your old horse could do with a rest. . . a long rest!' They all laughed, forgetting all their troubles in that brief moment of joy.

The coincidence of two Williams and two Sarahs was not lost on them, it created an impression of kinship, as in those days children were often named after their grandparents. Old Sarah made a fine fuss of young Sarah and the boys sat by the fire with their mother.

George, having seen the needy state of the farm, offered a day's work from him and the boys in return for the hospitality.

'Gladly accepted George my friend, gladly indeed. Sadly we were never blessed with children strong enough to survive their first years. We're getting older now and yesterday I strained my shoulder trying to keep a wayward ewe from jumping that broken fence you saw me struggling with. Sarah's not up to lifting heavy things either!' Old William smiled a knowing smile.

In the two days the Dinnicombe family finally stayed at the farm, situated not so many miles north of Challacombe, they transformed the place, fences mended, wood collected, chopped and stacked, barn hinges straightened and replaced, weeds cut, water fetched, roof patched. It was a hive of activity, a gloriously happy time, but then it was time to leave. George was destined for a somewhat different future.

The morning of their departure, old William the farmer, with his wife close by, spoke quietly and sincerely to George, 'George, you can see the future this farm holds for someone younger, we have no living relatives, no children to take over when we are gone. We would like to offer your boy William a home with us, treat him kindly like one of our own and one day he will be the farmer here.' Old Sarah held her hands together in hope and Phoebe's hidden hand pinched her husband's arm.

George understood the offer well enough. George had already decided what he must do, he could not give up his child as he had been. 'In my heart I cannot do such a thing, though I feel the kindness of your words and sense your loss as if it were my own. We must move on and leave you with happy memories and a knowing you will not be forgotten. But our destiny lies elsewhere.'

As they gathered at the farm gate, prepared to leave and say goodbye, Old William warned George of bad weather to come, 'Winter's not over yet George, the wind from the East and the colour of the morning's sunrise tell me that it's possible we may have snow. . . the moor is no place for anyone when that happens. You are always welcome back here if it proves to be too hard going.' Their hand shake was deep in the meaning of lasting kinship.

'Don't worry, William, we shall be fine, two days at most and we'll be off the moor and be on the sheltered wooded lowlands,' assured a confident George, a most able man in his mid thirties and with great strength and energy.

They walked with the horse to the top of the slope, only young Sarah hitching a ride on the back, waving her many goodbyes to the dear old lady who'd been like the grandmother she never knew.

William and Sarah Beer stood together as they always had and waved until the cart and all were gone from sight. They walked slowly back to their house, their minds filled with the dreams of what could have been.

The ancient track was still passably visible and in general followed contour lines or ridges. They were making good time until a trial of nature blocked their path. A small but unavoidable valley, evident from the reed growth and sphagnum moss that spread some twenty yards or so across the valley bottom, was the sort of marshy challenge they could well have done without. 'Everybody off the cart, even you Sarah, lift off some of the heavy things and we'll come back for them,' George was still confident it could be done, but oh for a stronger, younger horse. It was almost as much as Molly could do to lift her feet out of the bog, never mind pull the cart, which action only made her hooves sink deeper. 'Come on boys, hands to the wheel spokes, and you too Phoebe,' called George enthusiastically as he heaved at the harness and encouraged Molly to do her best. She was a willing horse and deserved no flogging. The wheels wobbled side to side with their worn bearings and rocked back and forth as the cart teetered on leaving a deep rut. With rests, it must have taken the family a good half an hour to place the cart on firm ground again. It was obvious that Molly was now lame. Experience told George it was probably a tendon in the lower leg, the swelling had already started, she might be able to hobble on for a while but pulling the cart would probably kill her. It wouldn't be the first horse he'd seen broken winded with age and excessive labour. There was little shelter in this valley of mostly grass and dead bracken though it was less windy than on the tops where the east wind was beginning to carry sleet. The sky was that peculiar grey that had the smell of snow.

'Right Phoebe, we must be a good seven or maybe even eight miles on from the Beer's farm, perhaps over the next ridge there may be another. Shelter as best you can in the cart, I'll be as quick as I can to fetch help.'

Phoebe noticed the change in George's voice, she knew he was worried, she knew that they should have heeded old William's warning and now their very lives were in God's hands. Sleet began to fall more heavily as George, collar up and leaning into both hill and wind that now conspired so cruelly against him, slowly clambered from sight. Phoebe prepared the contents of the cart as best she could to make a shelter, she leaned against the woodworm riddled side and gathered her children close, Sarah on her lap and the boys each side, pieces of sack cloth and a sheet of old darned canvas their only protection from the east wind's determined onslaught. The cold, hunting wind howled through gaps in the cart's sides and the torn canvas flapped noisily about them.

Phoebe knew only too well the truth of the matter, not all of them would live through this storm, but she reassured the children that all would be well, that their father would not let them down and would never leave them alone on the moor. She knew he would always come back, nothing would stop him.

Molly, now free from her traces and lightly tethered, stood resolute with her back to the biting wind and the sleet that slowly changed her grey to white, there was only one thing she was waiting for and it didn't disappoint. It wasn't long before she sank quietly to the ground, unnoticed, her work forever over.

George reached the summit with failing visibility but sufficient for him to view the surrounding empty moor. In front was another small valley, it shouldn't take him long to cross it and see if here was a farm the other side, or perhaps a shelter wood. He pushed himself harder than ever, his feet numbingly cold through the worn-thin soles of his boots. The touch of cold sleet pained his hands like a burning from the forge, his hands lost so much control he could no longer close a button nor adjust his collar. He knew as well as Phoebe, that they would not all survive this storm but he was not dead yet and he must find help for his family. 'Just one more hill,' he promised himself, and with fading hope, 'just one more hill.'

Meanwhile the sleet had turned to snow, big snowflakes riding the wind towards him faster than galloping horses, almost pretty to watch, practically hypnotising. . . George shook his head from his strange but passing fascination and pressed on.

Back at the cart, Phoebe's mind was in turmoil, what if George did not come back in time, even if he did will they still be strong enough to move? She thought about Mr. Beer's generous offer to care for her eldest boy, William. Possibly seven miles back to the farm it was, but young William was a strong boy, well nourished and big for his age, he had the determination of his father and the spirit of his mother. She made her decision. Daylight would not last forever, maybe four or five hours left, if William started out now, while still able, with the wind at his back and before the snow deepened he could make a determined one way hike to the farm before nightfall. Phoebe gently lifted Sarah, who appeared to be sleeping quietly now, to one side, she took off her coat and made William put it on, she wrapped him up well and asked him, 'Tell me William, do you think you can follow the way back to the farm?' William was sombre but nodded back in reply. 'Then off you go with my blessing, may God be with you and guide you all the way safe to the Beer's farm,' she kissed his cold forehead, pulled his cap down tight and helped him off the cart. 'Don't you stop,' she said, 'if you are tired you do not stop, you keep going, say hello to them and we send our love.' 'Don't you stop William. . . whatever happens, you keep going!' she shouted after him.

William turned, nodded again and was gone in an instant, he felt very grown up that his mother entrusted him with such a journey. . . he would not fail her.

Sheltered by two coats, with the cold wind at his back blowing the snow past him, his path was clearer, his body warmer and his intention resolute.

Phoebe settled back in the cart as best she could, already little Sarah the youngest was sleeping the long sleep, Thomas huddled closer, his shivering telling Phoebe he was still alive, she pulled the canvas and sacking tight around their bodies and quietly prayed, first for Sarah, then for William, Thomas and for her brave George, wherever he was, and only then for herself.

George's mind was confused, he was still walking but no longer sure in which direction, for snow had covered the ground and filled his footprints. He'd long since stopped shivering and was so tired he desperately needed to rest. Then astonishingly through the curtain of snow, like an apparition, came another man. The other spoke and beckoned him on. Though George could not hear above the wind, bemused, he followed the stranger to a small cob built shepherd's shelter, it had a simple but adequate heather thatched roof, and best of all a small fire of Gorse wood burned at one end. The host explained that he was a local shepherd looking for lost sheep before the blizzard took its icy grip upon the moor. George, unable to recognise his rapidly worsening condition, replied in a slurred voice, about his family needing help. The shepherd told him of a small farm two miles further east just off the ridgeway track. Though pleased with the news, George again felt extraordinarily drowsy. He took off his big coat to warm it by the fire and promised himself a few minutes rest before pressing on to the farm. Just a few minutes, that's all, it wouldn't hurt. In a moment he fell fast asleep, it never occurred to him that even if he reached the farm he was still lost, he would never find the cart again in this storm.

It was in that same instant that Phoebe ceased praying for his return. Hope and breath lay themselves peacefully down in the snow with the old grey horse, innocents all to the worsening storm.

George snapped awake keenly, his eyes acclimatised already to the dazzling whiteness about him. Feeling refreshed and comforted, with what he assumed had been only moments of rest, he glanced about him to see the shepherd had gone and the cob walls of the shelter now just snow lined remnants. George set off with renewed determination towards the farm the shepherd had described, his mind not in any state to question the events of his journey. He reached the farm with seemingly little effort. His hands no longer burned with the pain of cold, his footsteps were light and easy. He reached into his pocket for the one gold coin he had, the guinea Mark had given him. He would use it to buy help for his family. His closed fist knocked heavily on the solid farm house door but it remained closed. Twice more he beat on the door and called out in pity for someone to come. In the great muffled silence of falling snow, the door remained steadfastly closed to his desperate pleas. He could stay no longer, something dear to his soul was calling to him from across the moors. He turned and ran westwards, quickly blending into the deepening and all encircling whiteness. He would never give up, all that mattered to him was out there, lost somewhere in a landscape that more often than not buried its secrets. A terrible sense of loss had captured his spirit, at this instant George knew he could never ever give up.

Postscript.
Date: 2016, the 6th March.
Somewhere out on the wild moors of the Exe, several miles North West of Challacombe stood a part-modernised farmhouse. It had been on the estate agent's books for several months. Remoteness and old wives' tales about ghosts had deterred potential clients, but today. . . success.

Fingering the keys of his modern Range Rover in his pocket, the estate agent smiled with satisfaction at the proud new buyers of Ashcombe Oak Farm, 'I just know you'll love this place, especially when you expressed excitement about buying a remote property with a ghost! The previous owners didn't mind either; they told me it's a kindly ghost, possibly that of an old shepherd that is recorded as missing, presumed lost on the moors. Quaintly it knocks on the door of the original part of the farm house if the snow falls deep. Lovely isn't it? When they opened the door there was never anybody to be seen and no footprints in the snow. People love these silly old wives' tales, makes the moors more romantic, more interesting, don't you think? Still, we rarely have much snow here nowadays.

Oh, I meant to say, when the previous owners added the new extension they had to lift some yard cobbles and guess what? They found a golden guinea dated 1779, most probably dropped by some careless rich chap. Perhaps there's more out there. . . here's hoping for you eh?'

**

Each winter, whenever snow lies thick on the moors and the wind blows fierce from the east, George returns, he is ever lost yet ever searching for his family. Sometimes he chances upon the caring shepherd again, in eternity seeking his lost sheep.

**

Did young William, the oldest child, safely reach the Beer's farm? Did he live happily, marry, have children of his own and inherit the Beer's farm?

We will never know. We can only trust, as did his loving mother at the time.

'So do we pass the ghosts that haunt us later in our lives; they sit undramatically by the roadside like poor beggars, and we see them only from the corners of our eyes, if we see them at all. The idea that they have been waiting there for us rarely crosses our minds. Yet they do wait, and when we have passed, they gather up their bundles of memory and fall in behind, treading in our footsteps and catching up, little by little.'

Stephen King

**

'Experience is one thing you can't get for nothing.'

Oscar Wilde

7

Games in the Morgue
(Based on a true tale, an attendant's practical joke)

The old morgue was separated from the main hospital by a stretch of rough lawn and some trees. With little financial reward or appeal to the heart, few attendants stayed there for long but none as short as young Gavin, a slight built and shy man in his first employment.

Big Norm (Norman, a 16 stone ex-wrester) had earlier been tricked by one of the pranks played by other morgue attendants who, we note, are often blessed with bizarre senses of humour. He made plans to execute his own merciless version and poor Gavin was in his sights.

The morgue was always kept cold to maintain the dead in the same condition as on their arrival. Inside the flat roofed, brick built and windowless building, there were the usual sinks and cabinets as well as a number of trolleys and tables upon which the deceased awaited their various futures.

Electric lighting had been installed but the electrician in his infinite wisdom, or shortage of cable, had placed the switches on the right hand wall quite a distance from the doorway. In consequence, any visitor, particularly at night, had to enter the building and grope their sightless way along the wall searching for the light switch with ever nervous but hopeful hands.

So it was with Gavin that winter's night when he was sent on an errand to the morgue. If one can say it, of a nervous man entering a room full of dead people alone at night, he was blissfully unaware - unaware of Big Norm waiting for Gavin's grop-ing hand in the dark - with one of his own. His nostrils filled with the smell of death and chemicals, Gavin's thankful hand brushed against the switch box. Then he felt a powerful icy hand silently grip his wrist in the graveyard darkness of his new found hell. Despite the enormous difference in size and strength, Gavin seemed to have no difficulty at all in extricating himself and with a blood curdling scream he was out of the door and gone into the night. He was never seen nor heard of again.

Big Norm so enjoyed telling that tale, reliving the moment with a beaming smile – that's how I came to know it. But there is more, more that he did not enjoy as much, his voice always a little distant in the telling, as if not absolutely sure he believed.

One night, when attending the morgue in the hours of dark-ness, Norm was to witness one of the corpse shrouds moving, accompanied by obvious sounds of life. Frozen in time he watched as the 'corpse' got up and spoke to him. 'God, it's cold in here,' the corpse said, 'what's the time?' Norman looked at the winter clothed man before him and hardly believing himself replied, 'It's about half past four. 'The 'corpse', becoming more animated, asked if there was any chance of a hot drink. It was only then that Big Norm realised he was speaking to a visiting relative of one of the morgue's more permanently dormant guests. He probably belonged to a group that required the dead to be accompanied for 24 hours before burial.

This realisation came as a great relief, for even ex-wrestlers of Big Norm's stature had limits to their bravado. 'Not a problem guv,' he replied, 'I can fetch you a hot tea from the staff kitchen when I return to the hospital with theses samples.'

Norm left the light on and crossed the old lawn to the hospi-tal, his shoes leaving tracks in the dew. As he made a tea in the staff kitchen he laughed and joked with some of the night staff about his unexpected experience in the morgue that evening.

'First I've heard of it, Norman, and I'm the one that books everyone and every thing into the morgue,' said the duty doctor, 'we've only got four in tonight, old Mrs Tynes from the cardiac ward, two from a car crash end of last week and a homeless chap the police brought in and are investigating. No visitors, no religious chaperones, nothing. . . all quiet on the morgue front tonight. You must have been hallucinating. What are you putting in your tea?'

Big Norm was the only one not laughing, which of course made it all the more funny to everyone else.

He went back to the morgue with his guest's tea. The Light was still on and illuminating four cold tables, four shrouds and four corpses. None of them got up to ask where their tea was.

Big Norm left the job shortly afterwards and took up a much safer occupation, he joined the fire service.

Tea was drunk with the living there.

**

*'Peace lies not in the world
but in the man who walks the path.'*
**

8

Red Pike Revisited

'It is well said of man that there is three of each of him,
That which he is, that which he only thinks he is,
and that which he had intended to become.' Kai Lung

Whilst meeting with several others one wet December day and enjoying the many comforts of the Bridge Hotel in Buttermere, it is the impression of the author that there may be considerably more to each of us than Kai Lung's three. Indeed, among the throng there were those whose company was an immense pleasure, those that could just be tolerated and those that, well, let's just say, gave him a lesson in spiritual humanity.

Humility and Ego can argue the point another day but this was a day for Soul and Spirit's pilgrimage.

All of them had been to Red Pike before, all except the Old Fellow, this being his first and potentially last visit. The Old Fellow understood that they would all climb together as a group, taking the original route forged by the Younger One some 15 years earlier in the treacherous snow and ice conditions of the time.

The Old Fellow noted them all being present for food and drink in the bar the night before the walk, they were all present when the barman offered his advice on the best route to take and they were all present when breakfast of the full English variety was served in the morning. He wasn't to be so sure they were all with him later that day when he suffered on a rain lashed Red Pike summit.

Having settled the hotel bill and made arrangements to leave his car in the car park for safety, the Accountant joined the Old Fellow at the car. He was donning his new waterproof socks and over trousers as it was already raining with a forecast of plenty more to come. Despite boldly claiming so on the label, the Old Fellow's walking boots were not in the least bit waterproof, hence, the special socks. Ready to set off, the old chap looked around to see who was with him. There was Courage and the old enemy Fear, Intellect and his bosom pal Dopey. Memory was there too, not as good as he used to be of course but had at least bothered to turn up. Why Memory was wearing rose tinted glasses, the old chap was only to discover later on in the day. Knowledge and Skill were there giving constant advice. . . even if not wanted and short on accuracy. He couldn't remember how many should be in the group, but if they weren't there for the off then they'd just have to wait for the Old Fellow's return. . . they'd surely be much the sadder for not being part of such a fine pilgrimage.

In the process of worrying that he had remembered everything, the Old Fellow had forgotten to take his woollen gloves from the car. Memory reminded him shortly after leaving the car park but Bone Idleness and Obstinacy talked him out or returning for them, 'Stick your hands in your pockets if they get cold,' they exclaimed, 'we're certainly not going back, not now.'

Those that joined the group across the strip of land that kept Buttermere from Crummock Water were immediately faced with a choice of divergent paths. Memory impatiently took the lead, ignoring Thought and Consideration. Soon a stone bridge took them over the fast flowing Beck from which wild ducks watched them file past. Here was a short delay while the Photographer snapped away at several self thought masterpieces. Memory was so confident he knew the way but Memory had only seen the place in snow!

While lost in Thought, the group passed thoughtlessly by several 'insignificant' side paths that led up and away from the lake side, Memory also discounted them, they just didn't look quite right, now if they'd been covered in snow!

The Observer amongst them, who, up to this point had merely gone along with Memory, noticed a group of competently equipped walkers striding along a suitably higher line up the slope. The Observer pointed this out to the group but Dopey and Obstinate ignored any possibility of their being lost.

As the far end of Crummock Water seemed imminent so did the dawning of their collective mistake. They were definitely on the wrong path, the waterfall of Scale Force was now a kilometre away, about six hundred feet of climb higher and to the West of their current position. Navigator and Intellect carefully studied the map and terrain and using the Old Fellow's compass calculated their position. Logic confirmed their suppositions as probably 95.66% correct in the light of known circumstances.

Dopey, gladly and without questioning, accepted the information and along with staunch and unyielding support from the Great Blunderer they avoided any unnecessary backtracking by squelching doggedly up hill through deepening bog land. 'A short cut, friends,' Dopey assured the disbelieving group. They could only thank the Gods that the Clever One had been in control of the group in the Army and Navy Stores when those magical waterproof socks were purchased.

When the group, united or not as the case might be, approached the lower reaches of Scale Force they met two younger walkers going in the opposite direction. Friendly and his pal Inquisitive inquired of directions and inspiration. Meanwhile Envy greeded after the fine map of excellent scale that the two walkers had in their hands, so much better than the 'tourist map of northern Europe' that his own seemingly psychotic group was using. While Fairness admonished Envy for such a blatant exaggeration and for Envy's grossly one sided view on life, Generosity and Kindness, inseparable lifelong friends that they were, planned to persuade the group into donating their map case and compass to those walkers who had so kindly helped them. (Tired, Cowardly and Hungry had plans for going backwards, back to the warm hotel and a bar snack, they schemed and tried to infiltrate the thinking of other group members throughout the trek). Memory was to have several blackouts on the climb, huge portions of the route were not recorded anywhere in the archives. As Memory wiped the driving rain from his rose tinted spectacles, others in the group glared daggers, for they had been led to believe this was an easy short walk by an over optimistic Memory. Only Compassion smiled kindly on Memory, 'Poor old Memory is losing his marbles already,' he thought.

They turned left at the head of the steep valley and ran head on into an unfettered wind that drove rain horizontally across the exposed tops, hitting the group like a stampede of frenzied sheep driven on by a rabid dog. Dopey, Grumpy and Obstinate pulled together to 'encourage' the group on the incessant steady slog upwards into an unseen but easily imagined future. The Photographer among them wasn't as keen on taking pictures by now, as he could take photos of rain and cloud anytime at home, however, occasionally Memory would give him a nudge, after all he needed all the help he could get these days.

It was a long forgotten, murderous slog to the top of Red Pike which the Devil had liberally sprinkled with a variety of rocks, some big to break your bones, some small to slip and slide beneath balding old boots. On the approach to the unseen but assumed still present summit, Hearing, never reliable at the best of times, stopped the group in their tracks. 'Listen. . . that sounds like a helicopter!' They all listened but the sound faded. 'There it is again,' shouted an excited Hearing, 'perhaps the mountain rescue crews are up here and if we find them we might get a lift.' Hopeful wanted to rush on ahead but Logic, ably assisted by a pair of knackered legs, held them back, after all, 'why did the sound of the rotors come and go?'

Hopeful was about to explain exactly why this should happen, all to do with sounds and clouds and rock faces etc, when again the sound of helicopter rotors loudly filled the air. Insight, Intellect and Logic with one voice said, 'It's just the toggles on the coat hood flapping in the wind and hitting the rucksack, that's all it is. Come on, no rescue for us, only our own, let's get going and get off this damnable rock.' The Old Fellow was beginning to feel the strain and on studying the map for the shortest route back to the hotel he noted that even with a magnifying glass the contour lines seemed to touch each other.

In about one kilometre they had to drop down more than two thousand feet. Logic pictured two thousand steps each one foot high. Logic too was beginning to lose his marbles as nothing on that hill resembled his dream, in fact nearly all steps sloped away and down and were invariably wet and slippery. 'Most interesting,' mused Inquisitive. 'I wonder if we'll make it all in one piece.' Doom and Fear cried in unison, 'I bet we don't!' Fortunately for them, Dopey, their self elected team leader, took a hint from Patience and Endurance and the treacherous slip sliding descent began in Ernest, (the first time Ernest had been a fully active member on this expedition). Cloud and rain obscured any useful observations on where the path was leading, only the path itself was visible to the Observer, and he wasn't a lot of use once the path divided in two opposite directions. Logic and Dopey stared at the map together, neither could make any sense of the terrain so they simply took the right hand path and kept quiet to the others about their concerns. Foolhardy pressed ahead dragging a reluctant Wisdom behind him. Soon they were to meet up with the two walkers 'going backwards', there was a hush as the Old Fellow made a short speech and a presentation of the map case and compass, after all, he had made what seemed at the time a dying resolution that he would not be needing them again. Just before the exchange the Old Fellow asked for confirmation that the path his group were on was the correct one and that it was clearly marked all the way to the bottom. Satisfied by the positive answers and the young lady walker pointing down into the clouds saying, 'Bleaberry Tarn is just down there, it's lovely, you can't miss it,' the two groups went their separate ways. One towards the cloudy heavens and one into the misty abyss, both in the rain.

Bleaberry Tarn duly came into sight, the group looked to Memory for a comforting affirmation that he'd been this way before. Memory could do no such thing, he couldn't remember being this close to the Tarn at all, perhaps that little path they'd passed by earlier was the one he'd taken all those years before while on the Young Chap's winter expedition. Dopey couldn't care a less, not at this point anyway he didn't, and pressed on, crossing a tiny stream and some soft black boggy stuff. Observer noted that there were very few footprints along this so called 'path'. Dopey and his old pal Ignorance were now in their element. It seems that they had an old family motto in mind, *'He who presses on blindly is never truly lost.'*

They didn't share this arguably wise thought with the group. Dopey had taken them into similar trouble on more than one prior occasion. After a knee creaking, tortuous, rain soaked and slippery descent of more than six hundred metres, suddenly Memory was back in business, he hadn't remembered much of that descent at all but here, where the path dropped through a gateway into a coniferous wood, it was crystal clear. He had been here before and it could only have been on the 'lucky winter expedition'. (So called, as they were simply lucky to survive.)

Finally, back in the hotel grounds, the Old Fellow changed into dry clothing in the car park while Hungry and Greedy salivated in anticipation of the hotel bar menu. Intellect was calculating whether driving all the way home that same day was a viable option, Logic wasn't too sure but Homely and Hopeful could see distinct possibilities.

The Old Fellow broke his year long and oft transient Palaeolithic diet yet again and enjoyed a meat pie and a drink of hot chocolate in the bar, Friendship and Gratitude said their goodbyes to the hotel staff and with modern sat nav to instruct them, they drove North in search of the South West. They were on their way home.

All was going well until the Old Fellow joined the M6 going south. Immediately there was no convenient lay-by or stopping place, the evil Cramp had awoken. Cramp had been a silent stowaway throughout the expedition contributing nothing to the effort but he knew how to hit the unwary when they could least do anything about it. Now Cramp was wide awake, excited and keen to join the Old Fellow and his friends. As the

Old Fellow's left leg was gripped mercilessly by Cramp and his pal Pain he noted that the next services were fourteen miles away. Despite trying everything he could, including trying to crush his leg with his hands, the vehicle was slowly drawing to a halt. To avoid being nudged off the motorway by some itinerant juggernaut, the Old Fellow resorted to the rain soaked hard shoulder and went for a short hobble and limp.

Somehow it worked and the rest of the journey was shared with Peace. Memory cleaned his rose tinted glasses ready to tell the tale to anyone willing to listen. Hearing, half heard some Jasper Carrot jokes on the radio and Dreamer and Happiness conveyed the Old Fellow's now quiescent soul homeward.

Now that's what I'd call a worthwhile pilgrimage. It's a team sacrifice that brings us all together as one, one breath, one mind.

You already knew this, for they must often walk with you too.

'He who only walks on sunny days, never completes his journey.'

9

The Last Painting

Blocked from using electronic surveillance by an international conglomerate **** ****** ** ***** [we dare not publish its name] the government's Psychoanalytic and Euthanasia Department had to find new ways of locating undesirables in the community. Population control was necessary in order to improve immigration rights. The removal of undesirables was in its experimental stages.

Under the auspices of a national painting competition for all ages, with thousands of great prizes, the department set out to examine the deluded artistry of the proletariat.

Deep in the sub basement of Instow Psychiatric Research Institute, one such interview was in progress. The unsuspecting artist thought he was there to receive his prize but the truth of the matter was darker than any shade of grey.

The senior psychologist, known only as Barbara X, was a specialist in neuron irradiation, a new technique used to remove or disrupt any undesirable neuron pathways in those who chose not to comply with government wishes. It was expensive but more effective than putting chemicals in the drinking water as had been done in the past. Her able assistant known only as Eric the Red, was well experienced in spotting 'nutters' despite having no formal psychiatric training. He put his success in landing this job down to the voices in his head and having a distant relative who once slept with the then home secretary.

'Here's the nutter's painting ma'am,' sniggered Eric as he placed a childish drawing on the interview desk. The colours were drab even in the flickering light of an out of date fluorescent tube.

'Let's have a look at this then shall we?' glared Barbara X over her glasses at the confused patient (prize winner). 'Mmm. A Moon: sign of a repressed aspect of self. I see you live alone. . . a sign of abandonment and rejection.' She twitched violently remembering being rejected by her own parents and sent to Elton boarding school, the initiation ceremonies of which still gave her nightmares. But she was okay, she'd passed all the tests to get the job; she was impartial to the nth degree. . . depending on circumstances. 'Ah, a blue Parakeet,' (just like the one the headmistress at school had dissected): an indication of restriction, being caged, loss of freedom, inability to speak freely.'

Barbara X paused for a moment, slipped another valium into her mouth and washed it down with something that looked like water but had a chemical smell to it. 'Oh *this* is good, trees, excellent, well done, the symbol of knowledge.'

The interviewee wished he had some knowledge, like what the hell was going on. . . what a strange way to critique his art. He thought, 'I bet Picasso wasn't treated like this.'

Barbara X continued, 'Sadly they are painted in the familiar Picassoesque-style: the trees are unrealistic and their design shows no hope of longevity; survival is minimal. Also, I wonder why you painted at night. Hiding something eh? Night symbolises death and the hope of rebirth – well we may be able to help you there.' She fingered a hidden syringe in the open drawer of her desk. 'It is evident that your overcoat is covering up your true feelings of self, either that or layers of fat which you have accumulated. Perverted obesity on such a scale indicates you are not processing your emotions.' Barbara X paused briefly, 'Your treatment is free at the point of use and funded by a totalitarian government in Europe, which I cannot name for security purposes. Don't you worry about anything, we'll see to it all.' She closed the folder and reached under the desk.

She pressed a buzzer and Eric re-entered the room flanked by two burly and peculiarly happy-looking psychiatric nurses. 'Angela, Ann, help Eric prepare this nutter. . . I mean *patient*, for neuron research. I'll complete the sectioning data later. If we are successful, and yes we do hope that we will have one live through it one day, then we'll transfer him to the isolation town of Ilfracombe to live. He'll feel at home there.'

The new patient was stunned into silence as they began to remove him from the interrogation suite.

'Don't over-chloroform him, Ann,' cautioned Angela, 'I'm not carrying him all the way down to theatre like the last one.'

Barbara X finished her drink and relaxed, toying with a shrunken head she'd nicked from her old school museum. She could hear a protesting, but suitably drugged patient, being lead away along the corridor. Behind him a happy Eric the Red was reading from his poetry book.

Be careful what you draw !

**

'Do not look where you fell,
but where you slipped.'

**

10

The Writer – All Souls Day

From childhood, Susan Richmond had one abiding ambition – to be a writer. However, life had conspired to keep her dream out of reach. . . until today.

Today was All Souls Day and she decided to write a story in honour of her parents, both of whom had been talented writers. Her father was an eminent archaeology professor and author of many great historical novels. Susie's mother was more of a children's story teller - skilled with the sort of beautiful bed time stories that forever remained as treasured childhood memories.

Tragically, both parents lost their lives in a house fire while Susie was away at university. She would have been nineteen back then, some thirty years ago. The fire officer's report to the coroner had indicated that her mother was probably dead long before her father had entered the burning building in a desperate attempt to rescue her. A futile but brave effort that would cost Susie both of her parents.

Susie had tried writing stories many times before but any worthwhile tale always proved beyond her.

'None the less, today's the day,' she vowed, 'of all my days this is it. This evening, the magic will begin.'

She'd heard somewhere that a ritualistic scene setting was the key that opened the door to great stories. Such rituals placed the writer's spirit somewhere unworldly, somewhere between heaven and earth, in a twilight zone where souls could exchange ideas.

During the day, she tidied the house until all her jobs were complete and out of mind. She then lay resting on her sofa, listening to Tibetan chants on a CD she'd come across by accident in a charity shop. She waited quietly for evening to arrive.

Susie placed a cushion on one of the kitchen chairs and a small electric lamp on the table. The house was otherwise shrouded in darkness. Then Susie brought out a lavender scented candle, a mug of herbal tea, a glass of red wine, some white copier paper and her best fountain pen with spare ink. She sat comfortably, satisfied that the ritual was as good as it gets, her back warmed by an open log fire. Across the table, she observed her own reflection in a dark kitchen window. As Susie stared thoughtlessly at her own reflection it amused her to see glimpses of her mother and her grandmother looking back. These brief apparitions pleased her, as she remembered those kind people. Susie smiled to herself, took a sip of wine and picked up her pen.

The clock on the wall tick tocked its sleepy song, the full moon showed itself briefly from behind the clouds and the world journeyed on relentlessly.

'Oh no, not again,' she sighed, realising that all she'd done was stare at the white paper. The paper, without judgement or emotion, simply stared back, as it had already done for the last ten minutes.

Anxiously, she stared wide-eyed into an unhelpful gloom and begged the heavens for help. Anyone's Gods would do, ancestors, angels, even the devil himself if they could only release her imprisoned spirit.

Then it arrived, a joyful spark of inspiration. She didn't need anyone's help after all. Indigo ink flowed freely from her pen, though not quick enough for the wonderful ideas that crowded into her mind. She was almost in tears with the hurry to scribble one thought down before the next one pushed it aside. Her pen frenziedly scrawled across page after page. The scented candle flickered benevolently as she reached out for a sip of tea. The fire at her back reminded her of sitting on her mother's lap and the warmth of her body while some enchanting story lured her into the strange world of dreams.

Susie's father had told her more than once, 'a story must always have a grain of truth, like the grain of sand in an oyster from which something beautiful will grow.'

Her own grain of truth right now was about never giving up hope, that everything must be possible if you only apply yourself wholeheartedly into the venture, for it is belief itself that gives rise to real power.

Reflections looked lovingly on from the window pane, the soft light from the table lamp and perfume from the candle flame effortlessly carried Susie's hand across the paper – a masterpiece in the making. In beautiful script, the writer's spirit indelibly crafted the essence of story in her mind – it was no longer a mystery. Her father's words again whispered to her soul, 'Never try and possess something, for it will in turn, imprison you.'

At last, she'd made it. She was completely at one with her story, a mistress of her own destiny. The story was good. No, better than good. It was exceptional and very few alive today could compete with its brilliance. It was a prize winner for sure. Totally original, with heroine, mystery, danger and eternal hope, it was all she'd dreamed of, ever since she could remember.

Finally she put down the pen and felt her body relax. Then, the strangest thing, she sensed her father standing behind her, hands light and kindly on her shoulders, like when helping with her homework as a child. His voice, filled with reassurance, 'There dear, it's not so difficult after all, is it?'

Susie was startled by a burning log falling in the fire place and illuminating the room with its eerie light, her tea was cold, the candle nearly out.

She looked down to admire her work. Blank white paper looked back, still waiting.

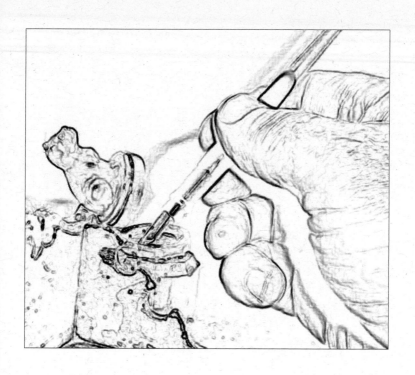

**

*'Of ghosts, as it is with mirrors,
only on reflection will you know what might exist.'*

**

*'The dream world has immense power that often will
not transfer to the waking world. In dreams there are
questions and answers of great intellect and intricacy far
beyond the wit of the woken mind that dreamed them. . .'*

**

11

Brain Conservation Trust Inc. USA
(Warning - not for the faint hearted nor the feeble minded)

Gordon 'Rhino' Wilberforce was a ruthlessly rich and unkind man who had enjoyed every minute of his selfish and abusive power. Now, age 74, aggravated by the belief he was dying prematurely he had plans, friends in the right places, and lots of money.

He sat up expectantly in his bed at the state clinical research institute, surrounded by the team he had carefully chosen for their ground-breaking work on neuro sciences and the fact they were all short of money, unable to attract government grants on ethical grounds.

Dr Hans Von Goering, probably the world's premier experimental brain surgeon, spoke first, in an American drawl with a tiny hint of German accent, inherited from his father. 'As we have discussed before, I can confirm that it is entirely possible to preserve the brain and its internal functions while separating it from the rest of the body. I have done this many times before, in conducting my own research with third world volunteers. We also have plans to include your heart as the pump for vital fluids, which we shall cull from suitable donors at a friend's laboratory.'

Wilberforce eased himself more upright, 'Why the heart then Goering, surely only the brain is important?'

Dr Goering smiled his charming salesman smile, meanwhile recollecting that the ancient Egyptians took everything but the brain to the afterlife. 'I believe the presence and connection of the heart will enhance the experience you will enjoy as you live out your dreams in perpetuity. This is an innovative advance in thinking, as often it is your heart that 'feels'. Your spirit flows between heart and brain, or mind, as we often call it. Just as you dream in sleep, so you will dream during induced stasis. You will truly feel a reality as you do in normal dreams, you will meet people, walk, run, shout. You will see colours, hear music and feel touch as though you were still connected to eyes, ears and hands. In some ways this reality will seem even more real and vivid than the one you are experiencing here now with us in this room. The so called heart-mind will improve your experience, you won't be sorry, trust me. The life force will be maintained and your soul will live on.'

Wilberforce nodded, feeling confident he'd picked the right man for the job.

Turning to a gaunt and spotty young man standing next to the doctor, Wilberforce enquired, 'is the electronic interface ready for use, Kosnitsov and how sure can we be that it will work as you suggest?'

Nikita Kosnitsov specialised in micro electronic implants and interfaces. He wouldn't disclose details but suffice it to say that the CIA was very pleased with his success rate. 'Have no fear, Mr Wilberforce, I have an excellent tried and tested design as used in medical neurology and have sourced only the highest quality materials. Your brain patterns will be under constant observation and will be recorded on a bespoke computer. . . with a secondary state of the art backup unit. I don't anticipate any problems with equipment or software, it is better than NASA use in their latest space technology. Changes in nutrient and fluids flow are automated and vary according to brain activity. If you fall asleep in your dreams then the system will tick over at an optimum rate for tissue longevity. During any highly active periods when you may be dealing in stocks and shares or some other splendid pleasure, extra nutrients are provided. We were wondering if you would like some drugs administered on a routine basis so that your brain could enjoy an enforced rest. Remember, we don't know if the isolated brain will follow a resting cycle or not, as it is the body that usually requires sleep, rest and recovery.'

Wilberforce shuddered as this was not something he'd thought of, he'd assumed that all would continue much the same as it did in his current life. 'What if things go wrong and I want to terminate the contract, how will you know?'

'Oh, you worry too much,' assured a tiny German accent, 'everything will be wonderful, I am confident of this, just like the life you have enjoyed, prior to your recent and untimely illness.'

It was a worrying concern to all parties involved should the contract be terminated. . . this was a good earner, not one to be sneezed at.

Nikita Kosnitsov youthfully reassured Wilberforce, 'Yes, please relax, be positive and have no fear, you don't want to carry bad feelings forward, I will install a failsafe monitored system that will deal with such eventualities, should the brain for some reason go into frenetic over activity across the whole neuro spectrum. We can terminate the nurturing process if suffering becomes evident within your dream reality. This should provide the safety net you seek.'

It was all gobbledygook to Wilberforce but he was impressed enough with Kosnitsov's spotty enthusiasm and collection of big words. He nodded his approval once more.

Last but not least was the owner of the clinic where Wilberforce's brain was to be interred. An oriental gentleman whose name Wilberforce failed to recognise let alone pronounce. Still, it was a new clinic and the owner had extensive business experience, running several companies in the past, including football teams, a bakery, two high class boutiques and a camel breeding farm. Wilberforce had seen photographs of the clinic's interior; it looked excellent, just like something from a tourist brochure on the Swiss Alps.

Everything was pre-arranged, Wilberforce would say a fond goodbye to his pretty, twenty six year old wife, Maryella, then the anaesthetic would be administered and the Doctor sign a death certificate – this would guarantee that Wilberforce's brain remained active, ensuring a seamless drift between the body life world to the undying dream world. It also cut out all the childish bureaucratic red tape associated with death and body disposal. As a final act of kindness to his two priceless Tasmanian Elk Hounds and knowing they could never be happy without their beloved master, they would be euthanized at the same time. As would his racehorse, Lucky Chap.

Wilberforce's last glimpse of life, through his own slowly blurring eyes, was to see his wife being comforted rather over affectionately by the good Doctor Goering. As the anaesthetic inexorably dulled his senses, the last words he heard were, 'Best you leave this to us now dear, try to think of him as dead, begin a new life, you are young enough to find a more suitable partner. Gordon will be happy where he is going; it was what he wanted, in fact deserved.'

Wilberforce's drugged ears faintly heard a door close, then the insensitive rattle of surgical tools on the trolley. Next time he would hear anything, would be in his new and long awaited dream life.

**

The stench of stale urine and tobacco smoke filled his nostrils, he felt a foot in his back and a gruff woman's voice startled him awake. 'Get up you lazy scum bag. Get up and wash the dishes, I'm not your blooming slave you know. Shocked speechless, Wilberforce obeyed and walked slowly barefoot down a flight of dirty and uncarpeted concrete stairs, the only benefit was that the air there was slightly cleaner. 'So at least it's not me that stinks,' he muttered to himself. He winced in pain as he trod on something sharp. Looking down he watched as a trickle of blood came from under his toes. Accompanied by a blood curdling scream, a dysfunctional child of about eight years old, ran at him and tore at his bleeding foot to recover a broken toy car, 'You stupid man, you've bust my car. . . I'm going to tell ma on you, you see if I don't, you big waster.'

Just like in any of our own dreams, understanding arrives without need for explanation. He knew this was his child, he just knew, just as he knew that the second child, aiming a catapult at him from the lounge doorway, was also his.

**

Meanwhile, in the living world at the 'Swiss clinic', a downtown industrial unit backing on to an oriental takeaway shop, Gordon Wiberforce's dreaming brain was settling in to its new surroundings. - None of which were as salubrious as the image to which he'd earlier and happily committed his wretched but hopeful soul. Nikita made the finishing adjustments to the equipment he'd bought at a bargain price on ebay and the doctor topped up the fluids reservoir with some waste plasma he'd been given by a friend at the local hospital and who owed him a favour. (Some say, another convenient death certificate, some just don't dare to speculate.)

**

In his squalid accommodation in a 1960s Bronx slum, Wilberforce continued to live out his nightmare. His brain allowed him to dream within a dream and in consequence he lived a weird form of double life. During his waking dream hours he knew the pains of hunger, the misery of unemployment, poverty and suffered the constant nagging from an overbearing, overweight creature which he couldn't believe he'd married. He was convinced he was ill. He had headaches and hallucinogenic flashbacks, (though his wife's cooking and drug habits may have contributed to those). He desperately needed to see a doctor, but none would entertain him without money or health insurance. Life seemed to be deteriorating apace. Both children had fleas or worms, or perhaps both. One day a knock at the door brought him premature hope, only for it to be dashed to pieces by she who stood in the open doorway blocking out the smoky city daylight. His wife's mother had come to live with them. 'Don't just stand there you dim witted animal, take my bags and my precious little Gordy. . . don't you dare drop him either,' she demanded as she thrust a grimy cardboard cat transport box into his arms. 'Now get out of my way. . . where's my little angel?. . . and with that she pushed Wilberforce to one side with the strength of a Russian shot put champion. The first thing the fat, long haired and flea ridden cat did when released was to urinate on a month old pile of Wilberforce's unwashed clothes. After that, it was all downhill.

Wilberforce's other dream, deeper still within his induced dream existence, was equally strange but at least contained some vestiges of a decent life. He often found himself in a fine mansion, usually looking for something. There were photographs and paintings of him with a pretty young blonde woman on a yacht and, what looked like him enjoying better health with two huge dogs. However, he never came across a living soul as he searched this grand house. The mansion was full of earthly treasures, many he could pick up and carry with him. . . until that is, his beautiful dream was broken by a scream or foot in the back. He could never bring even the smallest prize back to his Bronx slum way of life. If only he could, it would solve all of his problems.

**

It wouldn't be too long before big problems turned up in the real world, at the industrial unit - brain storage department.

Dr Hans Von Goering and Nikita Kosnitsov were urgently summoned to an emergency meeting by the new manager of the takeaway. Apparently the owner with whom they had formed a lucrative association, had used an alias in an attempt to shake off the tax collectors and had, not to put too fine a point on it, disappeared.

Von Goering was livid, such inefficiency warranted a firing squad, 'at least the brain is still being monitored. . . Well, it is, isn't it?'

The look on the manager's face said it all. 'One of the new boys was checking the monitor when all the instruments went crazy. There was a post it note on the screen saying, "When brain over activates, switch off." So he did.'

Nikita Kosnitsov was first through to the second hand kitchen cupboard where the brain was kept, he noted signs of biological decay and for all his efforts he could not reengage the interface. 'It's knackered. . . nothing we can do. Now we will lose all future instalments on the contract. We're done for.'

The manager, with yet another unpronounceable name, chimed in, 'What if I can get you another brain that looks like this one? There's a homeless guy, with a very sad life who sleeps in the alley. No one knows nor cares about him. It easy... we give him good supper first.'

By the end of the evening the new brain was installed. Gordon Wilberforce's out-of-sell-by-date brain lay dormant on a work top. 'Can you find a use for this?' asked Von Goering, 'and can you find some suitable fluids to top up the reservoir?'

The new manager was always ready and distinctly able to please, this would be the beginning of a profitable relationship.

**

Gordon Wilberforce had been an intelligent if ruthless man in life and having no need of body rest continued to study his dilemma night and day – whatever that means in the world Wilberforce inhabited. Slowly he had come to terms with his awful dream life while finding ways of spending more and more time in the dream within a dream. So much so that it was becoming his new reality. Now young and healthy, he advertised for staff for the mansion, an attractive young woman called Maryella applied and he was soon enjoying a relationship with her. The telephone rang frequently with offers of investments and a friend called with two large puppies. Tasmanian Elk Hounds apparently. Wilberforce in a brief and ironical moment of enlightenment realised that he was free... plasma swirled in an excited flood through his euphoric, racing brain ... then, it all went dark... forever.

**

Now, you may think this a somewhat distressing tale but ask yourself, 'Who is there that was not relieved of their suffering i.e. made happy?'

Gordon Wilberforce learned a valuable lesson on what it was like to suffer for a change but then found enlightenment and immortal happiness.

Pretty Maryella found new joy in life and to her dying day believed that her husband had found what he'd wanted.

Dr Hans Von Goering used the money from Wilberforce's trust fund to further his valuable neurological research.

Nikita Kosnitsov went on to develop robotic systems controlled by brain patterns, being later awarded the Nobel prize for science.

The manager at the takeaway shop kept faith with the homeless man's brain, which enjoyed a far better reality than when sleeping rough and painfully being ostracised by humanity. (And he'd been blessed with the finest last supper anyone could wish for.) The takeaway business thrived and has become one of America's most popular brands.

The oriental gentleman succeeded in escaping the tax collector and went on to start many more small businesses, giving hundreds of young people opportunities they wouldn't have had without him.

Even the dream dysfunctional family were happy in their own way.

Don't be sad, in the end every one was happy. Think about it.

"Trust in dreams, for in them is hidden the gate to eternity."
Kahlil Gibran

**

'What we deeply cling to imprisons us.'
**

12

Meditation – one last journey.

Using meditation, Tom had found a way in which he could leave his pained and frail body behind in the hospital bed and visit the mountains he'd always loved. Once there, he was fit and strong, his breathing easy. His favourite journey was to walk from the wooded valley and beyond the tree line to the sun bathed snow slopes above.

While enjoying his mountain walk one day, he was overwhelmed by an urge to know what lay the other side of the summit. He'd never ventured that far before and knew he must delve deeper and longer than ever. Deeper still into the quiet of his inner consciousness he went, until at last, just a few more steps to take then he would be on the other side, a place he'd never been before. He knew he dare not stay long for soon it would be time to return to his miserable existence of pain and distress.

**

It was just after three in the afternoon when Doctor Gratton solemnly addressed grieving relatives gathered at Tom's bedside, 'I'm sorry to say we've lost him. We tried everything we could but found no response. I'm afraid we were left with no alternative but to terminate and switch off the machine. He seems at peace now.'

They nodded in acceptance that Tom would no longer feel pain.

**

A stillness filled the room, much as he'd always found on his mountain.

**

'One thought alone can stop a thousand.'

**

13

The Traveller's Confession.

Aged 84 he'd run his course and he knew it; his bones were old and weak. A kindly fire warmed his life-tired body and what he knew would be his last supper. He'd learned the hard way how to leave the dearly beloved behind him and never return, never to tell. He'd been no stranger to loneliness, though it hadn't started that way.

His old horse was now tether free in the field and would doubtless find a good home, such was his nature; as would his old dog, noble companion for some six years now.

As he gazed through the light smoke at his faithful old dog, he wished such loyalty had been part of his earlier life. However, now was the time to tell what had remained a secret these forty years.

'Well, my dear old pal,' John said quietly, as if others might overhear, while his dog obliged by cocking an ear and tilting his head to one side. 'My early years were bathed in riches and privilege. We had a grand house in Belgravia and vast estates in Mayo. Life was good, I knew no other. I married, we had a lovely son and we had servants to look after us. It was one of them that changed my life. She had come by some gossip of which I'd known nothing, nor could I entertain. She threatened to disclose an affair between my mother and a traveller who frequented our lands in Mayo. True or not, to protect my mother and the man I knew as father, as well as my own wife and son, she had to be silenced. In silencing her, I was overwhelmed by consequences that simply hadn't occurred to me. I had to run, so run I did. I made my way from Belgravia to our country estate in Mayo which I knew so well from childhood days. I found the old traveller that I'd often seen watching me in those early, care free childhood years. I spoke with him; it was easy unburdening my worries on a stranger with no connections to courts, police or what we foolishly call civilised society. He understood, he was kindly and he took me in, he showed me the ways of the traveller. In truth he was to me as good as any father could be to a son. Before he breathed his last he asked me to break with tradition and not burn his caravan. For I was to use it and safely live out a worthy life as best I could, knowing travelling was in my blood.'

The fire was dying and he no longer felt like eating supper. He would light a candle and rest in his bed and dream of better days and what could have been. He stood shakily and patted his old dog gently on the head, 'Some things are sadly missed in life. . . sadly missed indeed.'

   As the mists of morning rose, the faithful hound lay quietly by the still warm embers of a once proud traveller's caravan and in the ashes Lord Lucan kept his secret still.

**

'Faith is the bird that knows the light
while the dawn is still dark.'
**

14

Holiday by the sea – freedom at last

*This is the tale of a man who has rented a house near
the sea but an unexpected storm is brewing.*

Soon the tide rising against the cliffs would isolate his accommodation from the village. A village in which he had found no hospitality, only hostility and a darkness of intent as well as approaching night.

With nowhere else to go and with ever growing fear as his only companion he realised his rented house at the end of the causeway was his last resort.

As he approached, he wished that he'd not dropped his bottle of wine on the cobbles earlier. If nothing else it could have proved a useful weapon against the unknown and unwelcome visitor that he'd just seen staring at him out of his own window.

With heart pounding in his chest and legs all ashake with adrenalin, he turned the door handle quietly. The quieter he was the worse were his fears. He reflected that he should have entered with a shout and a pretence that he was not alone.

He was not alone. As his hand searched for the light switch, a voice from the darkness said, 'Wait, please don't be putting on lighting, let me close shutters first.' It was a soft, kindly voice, a young woman's voice, with an accent.

He paused a moment, now not so afraid and as the wooden shutters clicked closed he asked, 'who are you, what do you want, why are you here?'

Her soft voice, now with a stronger accent, possibly Russian, told him it was all clear to put on the light. The light now on,

all his fears melted away along with his heart, for she was most attractive and seemed completely at home in the house he had rented for the week. 'Let me explain,' and with an adorable smile, 'we normally use this house ourselves, you are as much a surprise to us as we to you.'

'We? Us?' he thought, with diminishing hopes of sharing the young lady's company with no one else but himself. 'And why the secrecy? Why keep the house in darkness?'

'Oh, don't worry about anything,' she smiled again, 'our friends will not be stopping long. I prepare big feast for them, traditional food to make them feel welcome. Here, try some of this special pepper vodka I have brought with me.'

After a few glasses of eastern rocket fuel, which he'd never have accepted off any other stranger, he felt better as the now-delight-of–his-life busied herself in the dining room. He was hungry to be sure and the lack of food had increased the effects of the foreign strength alcohol.

He hardly noticed a burly bearded man with wet sea-boots enter the room and usher in about a dozen young men of obvious foreign origins, also sporting wet feet.

A few more vodkas later and he was sitting amongst the revelling group, enjoying a laugh – even if he didn't know why. The table was full of food and he hadn't eaten all day. The pretty one would touch his shoulders as she filled his plate with 'especially for you' morsels.

'Oh, this is heaven,' he thought, 'such good company, fine drink, good food and a friendly pretty lady.' Ladles of spiced tripe and various other unrecognisable entrails were dolloped into waiting bowls, hurrying hands reached out for roasted duck gizzards and eager mouths sucked brains through the eye sockets of fish heads – and strangely – he didn't care.

Vodka-infused euphoria, along with the attentions of the prettiest girl on the planet, made him happy at last.

He was woken by a heavy thumping on the front door; he staggered wearily through the quiet, now deserted, old house in darkness. 'Perhaps she's locked herself out,' he thought – but it wasn't to be.

'Armed Police,' came an authoritative, just-make-a-move-and -make-my-day, voice. 'We've been watching this place for months. We have a warrant to search your transit house you filthy slave-trading scum.'

*

Still not at all sure of what was happening, he listened to the two men in the front of the car as it sped him towards an interrogation cell – somewhere in a damp sound-proof basement no doubt. 'Oh he's Russian Mafia all right, we found a signed photo of Olga Killamov, code name Red Bimbo, in his pocket saying, 'Thanks for everything - you were wonderful.'

His nasty looking pal replied, 'He'll soon be squealing like a pig, the evil swine that he is – I can't wait to ask him a few questions once he's wired up to the mains. He'll soon stop thinking about pretty Russians by the time I've finished with him.' They both laughed – and not a happy laugh either.

He sank deeper into the back seat, eased his wrists in the handcuffs and dropped the empty pepper vodka bottle he'd been cradling, and thought, 'What a bloody awful holiday, it'll be Butlins for me next year, or Cuba sounds nice.'

**

'Your mind will play tricks on you – your spirit won't.'

**

15

Last desperate grasp for fame

Ever since leaving school, she'd wanted to write and write well: to please, to entertain, to enlighten. All too often her proud efforts were denigrated by the blindly opinionated, but she never once let go of her dream. Her soul burned with the desire to produce a literary masterpiece that none could, nor would ever dare deny. . . a lasting and fitting epitaph to her life struggles and final triumph.

'One day,' she determined quietly and resolutely to herself, 'one day.'

Week in week out, year in year out, in respectful humility she applied herself to researching, thinking, scribbling and typing her short stories. Slowly changes came, in her style, in genre, in grammar and in composition, though few credited her efforts.

Eventually, as old age beckoned her more assertively, inspiration came at last, a 'light bulb' moment, a brilliant story like she'd never heard before. . . an original. The story burned like a bright light in her soul, illuminating all that was once hidden in darkness.

Soon after, in a secluded cliff top hut overlooking the Ocean she was to find the perfect setting to entrust her mind's eye to the written word and finally reveal her true literary genius to the world. Life had never before felt like this. She was enchanted.

Keeping the dark wooden window shutters in place with the door open to sea and sky, her sanctuary wore the quiet cloak of a hermit's cave. It was ideal, only her, her pen and her ideas. Even the little path outside remained peacefully quiet and un-walked all day. It was a most appropriate place to begin and end her story. A story that couldn't have been finished any where else.

With a simple, admirable character, succinct wording and in-dispensable description, her story was as good as any could ever pen. Her little hands struggled to make the pen move quickly enough over the paper. The spelling was rushed and flawed, but no matter, the story and its final twist transcended all criticism. No one would dare venture a word of disparage-ment over this one. Once typed up correctly at her leisure, it would be sent out to eagerly awaiting publishers. She knew it would be a success and they would fight over the rights like their lives depended upon it. At last she would be known, be valued, she would be somebody, her name would live forever along with the Bronte sisters, Austen, Potter and others. Her efforts and enduring faith in herself would finally be vindicated.

As the tide withdrew for the second time that day and dusk tentatively approached, her cramped fingers scrawled the final, spidery, inspirational line - a line exclusively sent her by the Gods.

Now it just needed taking home to type. Pulse racing, her heart almost burst with excitement as she tore her story pages from the pad. She stood and walked to the door, a half step out-side and, feeling dizzy, she paused momentarily. She reached a hand out for the shifting door frame.

'Silly me,' she thought, 'must have been sitting too long.'

The thought had hardly left her mind when she was struck by a thudding chest pain. Her left hand tightened to a fist re-luctantly crumpling her precious story. She was still conscious as her body hit the uneven slabs outside the hut and felt the cool of an evening breeze begin to blow.

Later, in the unattended moment of her passing, her hands twitched in one last desperate attempt to hold on, then relaxed and fell open.

A passing dog walker discovered her body next morning. Her literary gem, her epitaph, the proof of her worthiness was already scattered by the four winds into oblivion and, just like so much other litter, blown along the distant shoreline.

Only nature herself knows she was worthy of her own belief and yes, you're right, we don't even know her name.

"Anything that can be lost, was never truly yours".

**

No one knows what is in your head – even you cannot be sure!'

**

16

Beware the Devil

All you will find about this particular case in the public domain is a heavily redacted Coroner's report with its innocuous conclusion - 'Death by Misadventure'. The victim's only living relative was his mother and after her son's bizarre and tragic death, she lived in a secure mental institute with little hope of release. Police, medics, and the undertaker were all sworn in to the Official Secrets Act and the press were gagged by a 'D' notice. Even the lone attendant at the crematorium was bound to secrecy. However, the horror to which they had all been exposed was in itself a more compelling reason to keep it quiet than any threat from the authorities. They'd take this awful 'knowing' to their graves. . . if they ever dared to die!

What I am about to tell you must remain a secret. If you are nervous or superstitious, then don't read on.

It was coming up to Halloween in a small market town some-where in rural England. We shall call the deceased, Tom, and his mother, Rowena. Tom had grown up as a rather awkward child, a little devil he was at times, possibly missing a fatherly influence and taking advantage of an over-tolerant mother. Rowena was hard-working and kind, probably too kind and she indulged Tom with almost anything for which he asked. Rowena often wondered if he was suffering from one of those modern ailments with which doctors liked to label children. Not like the old days when they were told they were slow, thick or just trouble making and the remedy was punishment by slipper or cane.

Tom only had a few friends at school, all eccentric. . . with quite odd senses of humour, but Tom's time at school was coming to an end – in more ways than one.

The more Rowena tried to make him realise the seriousness of finding work the more Tom rebelled and stayed in his room, pursuing whatever amused him on the internet. Tom loved the practical joke videos of people being surprised, shocked or even frightened. How much he wanted to do the same thing.

One night, while browsing the internet he had a great idea. Oh, how it thrilled him. He would dress up as a ghoul and leap out from the churchyard on unsuspecting passers-by. He could easily run back through the grave yard and out the other side and be only two streets from home and safety.

All was ready, the eve of All Saints day had arrived. As normal for the season it was dark early and a hint of mist hung in the air forming halos around street lamps. He said nothing to his mother as he slipped out of the back door into darkness. The large churchyard with its ancient Yew trees was dimly lit by a single bulb over the church doorway, now always locked against thieves and rogues that sought a different type of sanctuary from their ancestors. Tom adjusted his baggy and cheaply hired ghoul suit and began to creep along the gravel path. He stopped abruptly at the sound of muffled laughter. . . worse still, it seemed directed at himself. Then he saw them, three youngish men also dressed in Ghoul outfits. . . but these were good. Oh, how he envied them. They called him over, and he went. On discovering what Tom was up to, they offered to join in and what was more, they could find him a spare suit, just like theirs. Tom couldn't wait. He discarded his own amateurish effort and donned the new ghoul suit, which fitted like a glove. It was perfect, easily good enough to fool a silly old pensioner or annoying child. He should be able to give them the fright of their lives. He laughed quietly in excited anticipation. Even better, his new found friends were keen to join him.

First victim was an elderly lady with a walking stick and a little shopping for her tea. She'd dropped her shopping bag and slumped forward holding her chest, at this the gang slipped back into the darkness of the graveyard. When the old lady had looked up again there was no one there, bemused, she had crossed the road and hobbled home another way.

Then there was a young man, perhaps from Tom's school, he'd been lost in a world of his own, listening to music on his phone, until the creatures from hell appeared suddenly in front of him. He turned and ran, he ran like the devil was on his heels, the demonic little gang chased him for a while until laughter got the better of them and they returned to the murk and safety of the grave yard.

Later in the evening there were fewer people out on the street and Tom noticed a police car at the end of the road. It was time to go home. Tom asked if he could keep the suit for another time, the three seemed reluctant to let him keep it, suggesting that it might not be a good idea. Then, as Tom pleaded desperately to become one of them, they changed their minds. Why not, he was good company, they could meet again.

The next day, Tom's lifeless body was found in the graveyard, still in his beloved new ghoul suit. Police identified Tom from the folded heap of his own clothing in which they found his address. The local newspaper printed a story about some idiot prankster wearing a Halloween costume and warning the public against the foolishness of such acts, which may even result in prosecution. The police appealed for witnesses to the lone prankster that had plagued passers by outside the Church grounds. They were not looking for anyone else in relation to the matter.

The full seriousness of this bizarre event only became apparent when the forensics people recovered the body. It was then that orders came from the very top. Under no circumstances was any of it to reach the public domain.

Rowena was mortified to hear about the death of her only son, 'He was a good boy', she assured herself, 'such a good boy.' Tom's body was held briefly at an isolation morgue used by forensic scientists.

Rowena was advised not to view the body as they could identify him through a DNA match. It would save her from a nasty

shock. If you wanted an understatement, that was surely it. She didn't listen.

A highly experienced pathologist, brought out of retirement for the purpose, could not determine a cause of death, he considered asphyxia, drugs, poisoning and more but in the end concluded that no known scientific reason existed for Tom's death. It was as though the light of life were simply extinguished - the lantern of life taken elsewhere to illuminate another world.

Tom's body was cremated at a very private ceremony, if one could call a hurried lone disposal at midnight a ceremony. He still wore the ghoul suit which in some strange way had stuck to him. It couldn't be removed, even by cutting, for all that did was cut into his body. His skin was one with the suit – it was his skin.

Despite counselling and medication, the nightmares never stopped for those who had witnessed this strange and awful truth.

By Christmas time, Rowena was sitting in a rocking chair at the institution, pulling at her clothes and skin and staring inanely into space. 'He was always such a good boy.'

**

'Beware the devil's invitation.'
**

17

Vladimir Maximus Ratsowski
Reluctant Stowaway

Based on the true story of MV Lyubov Orlova. In 2014 the ship was floating lost in the Atlantic, full of rats seeking new homes.

Soon coming to a beach near you!

They thought the old freighter was empty when the salvage vessel lost the tow in a wild Atlantic storm. Back on shore in the safety of his office on the thirteenth floor of MARINE PROFITEERS INVESTMENTS CORP the boss said, 'It's not worth the effort. Let it go, we have other fish to fry.' So the freighter, *Doomski of Bubonikar*, was let free to sink or roam as the case may be. They would never have said 'it's not worth the effort' if they'd known who, or rather what, was on board . . . and still alive!

Vladimir Maximus Ratsowski was king rat on board, weighing in at just under a kilo of tenacious life-threatening muscle and sinew. Vladimir was a tough cookie, born and raised in the dauntingly harsh docklands of an old north Russian commercial port, no stranger to fighting for the last crumb and now the first and last crumb were his for the taking. Oh, there were other rats on board but any that looked like they could become a challenger in the future were soon despatched by Vladimir and fed to his offspring. Vladimir had controlled the population with his daggered incisors even when food was plentiful. . . his plan was to stay on top. . . king rat, lord of all he surveyed and master and commander of his very own ship. *(Eat your heart out Russell Crowe – Vladimir would!)*. Summary assassinations were his tool of choice, and he was omnipotent.

After a few weeks adrift and with the storm abated, they had found the weak and dying body of a stowaway vagrant who had gone on board in search of a better life than the one he'd not enjoyed so far. Vladimir took advantage of fresh meat and made sure the stowaway stayed alive as long as possible while they gnawed away at the edges. For them it was like a Smorgasbord and trip to Disneyland rolled into one. Life was good . . . unless you crossed Vladimir's will of iron.

After about 3 months, even the bones were gone and to ensure his lineage continued Vladimir started to cull the pack and feed his family; the more power he and his family had the easier it was to exert even more power. There was an old rat song loosely translated from the Russian that went something like *'it's the rich what gets the gravy, it's the poor what gets the blame'* and Vladimir liked it even though it has to be said he didn't quite understand it. None the less his wife, Amelia, a pretty brown-eyed foreigner, sang the song with gusto, as did her children.

Six months went by and no ships or planes came close, bits started to fall off the ship, corrosion, lack of maintenance and storms were doing *Doomski of Bubonikar* no good at all.

Rats had a motto, *'It's an ill wind that blows nobody any good'* - Vladimir couldn't understand that either but he could remember it and that alone pleased him well enough. Ill winds would sometimes cause seabirds to shelter from the storm and land on the vessel. In thinking they would save their lives, they lost them. Stealthily in the night, Vladimir would take down every one. He enjoyed doing it; it kept him razor sharp and honed his formidable warrior skills.

Nearly a year passed and rumours on the mainland began spreading about this ghost ship with unknown cargo. . . and where it would find landfall. Governments began to question their options, 'Well it's not our problem yet. . . still international waters.'

'Let someone else do it, it will be cheaper. . . since the cuts, I'm not too sure we have any suitable aircraft in the UK, they're mostly on loan to some middle eastern country, er, can't remember which one now'. . . and so it went on.

At long last and driven by the Gulf Stream the *Doomski of Bubonikar* appeared off the Cornish coastline. Coastguard put out a warning, as did the Environment Agency, the press sent out warnings and the TV was full of it. Why was nothing being done?

Extract from a TV interview: 'We asked the Home Office, Ministry of Defence and several other ministers and Ministries to come on the programme, none were available for comment at this time but have issued this statement; 'Her Majesty's Government has been made aware of the proximity of a vessel approaching the Cornish coastline. We advise you to take heed of warnings put out by the various agencies and to monitor the news channels. The Government is doing all it can to confirm the name of the vessel and to contact the owners whose responsibility it is to make it safe. Since privatising the Coast Guard such matters are no longer the responsibility of the Government. Letters are being sent to local councils whose parishes border the coastline reminding them of their own duty of care.'

Our news team has ascertained that the Minister for Defence is holidaying on Freebee Island, popular resort and tax haven, and his deputy, A Morron MP KFC and Bar, said that the minister will set up an enquiry into the whole matter on his return next week.

Breaking news. . . Guernsey has located their military plane and would be pleased to blow up the ship in British coastal waters when given permission. We understand permission has already been granted by a surprised PM who was woken early from sleeping off an Eton old boy's reunion party. The *Doomski of Bubonikar* will be bombed and sunk when Guernsey has bought fuel for their plane, possibly on Tuesday when Morrison's do a promotional ten pence a litre off deal.

The vessel is currently drifting 600 yards from shore - a fit and determined rat can swim 3 miles. The lightly populated Cornish coastline is rugged and inhospitable, an ideal breeding ground for rats. Our best advice is, pray for an early death.

A junior spokesperson on an automated messaging system for the HSE said this was an unfortunate but unavoidable accident and their thoughts and prayers are with the families who live near the incident.

**

'Tomorrow does not exist.'

**

18

The Coroner's Verdict.
An Exmoor tale of intrigue.

*All names have been changed to protect the innocent,
that being me, (protection from litigation, prosecution,
kneecapping or simply being fed to the pigs).*

It wasn't so long ago, certainly in living memory; in a land where the pace of life and the people who lived it seemed to have been left behind by civilisation itself. Our story is inspired by a misplaced coroner's report, unfounded rumour, and an isolated moorland inn - we cannot say where. . . that must remain another secret.

The press, particularly the rural press, *Moonraker's Weekly* and the magazine *Cull Monthly*, were full of subjective speculation as only the press can do (anonymous sources) and the scattered moorland communities were rife with fervently bigoted rumour. Rumours without any basis in fact but none the less, they spread like bubonic plague. The series of Chinese whispers making them worse at each telling. Over garden walls, in the streets, the shops and pubs, everywhere rumours flourished. 'Of course, his wife will have to move house you know. She can't stay there, not now. I bet it was much worse than we can imagine. . . poor woman.' 'Yes, they say she must have known he was seeing them on a daily basis, probably calling out their names in his sleep; Must have been awful for her.' 'My God, I mean when did he go? Did he go at night? He always seemed to be around when we visited the inn. Nice bloke too, friendly chap he was.'

'Arr, that be his trouble, they'm reckons he were a bit too friendly they'm do, oo arr.' 'Why, I'd heard he even had a portrait or a sculpture of one of his old acquaintances brazenly displayed on the pub wall.' 'Arr, no, it were the real thing, it was a real pig's head, nailed to the wall above the fire place it were. . . girt big tusked thing, bold as brass he was.'

And so the rumours went on and on and still to this day if you listen with a hush you'll catch the whisperers at work whenever two moor-land people meet.

The coroner, a Doctor Remus Blenheim-Landrace Esq OBE, chairman of the local hunt committee and an internationally celebrated Cavy/Wallaby cross breeder, had concluded a misadventure verdict on the matter even before the matter had been investigated. He hadn't been interested in tittle tattle, well not publicly anyway, he dealt with evidence, hard evidence; he was a staunch right wing defender of the law, as he saw it anyway. Close friends of the good Doctor though, confided that he'd his own personal suspicions, about which he was bound by sacred oath not to disclose.

These are extracts from the personal diary of the court recorder, an elderly spinster with a vehement dislike of men. Miss Hades Vendetter always kept private notes as well as meticulous court records, that way she knew the truth could never be hidden. Sometimes she would feign deafness in order to humiliate a witness into repeating something she knew they'd rather not. 'Excuse me Coroner, could you ask farmer Cagey to repeat that bit about having a fondness for pigs himself, I couldn't hear through his mumblings, thank you coroner,' a hint of a snigger in her voice. The witness was then forced to face Miss Hades and repeat in loud clear words that yes he was a pig fancier and proud of it. The police had confiscated a number of computers from drinkers at the pub, there was no denying it, the hard drives said it all, deleted files couldn't save them from forensics. Several farmers were questioned as to why they had googled for things like, 'how to bed down your pigs', 'what pigs need to keep them happy', 'how to keep pigs quiet', 'the dangers of making one pig your favourite', 'nice names for pigs', 'alcohol and pig behaviour', 'pig breeding habits', and so on. They came up with several lame and obviously conjured excuses like, 'breeding pigs for meat', 'growing pigs on for market', etc, one foolishly admitted to owning a pot bellied pet. A senior Home Office Immigration official, Mr Ian Neptitude was contacted immediately as this pig was believed to be of Vietnamese origin and invoking even more scandal. There were a lot of people, high society people, who hoped the net wouldn't be spread too far and wanted the minimum of effort exerted in this tragic and obviously misunderstood case.

A top forensics scientist, Dr Joseph Scraghill PhD, JP, holder of People's Star of USSR, and a closet communist, had been given the investigation by accident. On the governor's desk two pieces of paper lay one over the other, one said, 'Do not employ this man on anything important'. The other piece of paper was instructions for an all expenses paid 'holiday' trip to Exmoor on a job that 'didn't warrant close inspection'. Scraghill's name was inadvertently scribbled on the wrong one by a work experience girl from Bulgaria. Dr Scraghill couldn't understand why he'd been given such a plum job and looked upon it with scepticism and a great deal of suspicion, 'they'll have to get up earlier in the morning to catch me out,' he thought, planning the most detailed investigation since helping the KGB and the Stasi finding covert capitalist scum during his annual summer holiday trips to the old eastern block.

Well now he was in the witness box in front of Doctor Remus Blenheim-Landrace Esq OBE, a man to whom he instinctively took an intense proletariat dislike and if the country was run his way he would have had him shot at dawn - or earlier.

The coroner hadn't got a clue who he had before him, he was half asleep and mentally writing his concluding speech, in a beautifully vague whitewash colour. . . 'Er, welcome Doctor, I understand that you are the so called expert witness sent by Whitewash. . . I mean Whitehall.

'Not exactly Doctor,' glared Dr Scraghill as if looking along the sights of an AK47, 'I am the forensic scientist in charge of the investigation and will be giving you precise and definitive evidence relating to this bizarre suicide.' There was a gasp and shudder throughout the court and public gallery, from whence the occasional whiff of silage would flavour the air. Now the coroner was no longer half asleep but with eyes bulging out he stared disbelievingly at the perpetrator of such sordid lies about his friend and brotherhood associate, the deceased.

'We'll see about that Doctor, please proceed with your illusory suppositions,' said the coroner whose voice had suddenly reverted from his Devonian accent to one that was more often found in the dormitories of Eton, 'please proceed and with all due caution Doctor.' He wondered if his advantageous coroner powers extended to prison terms for despicable witnesses. . . or having him sectioned might be better, cleaner, clandestine, less paper trail, yes the Doctor might enjoy seeing what it was like on the other side of the wire so to speak. Wouldn't do him any harm at all.

The coroner came out of his day dream just as the witness continued. . . 'wire, yes wire was used in the most intriguingly clever manner for such a mundane man as a pub landlord, very clever. From what I have gathered the landlord was inclined to beer drinking binges with his pigs, who he apparently knew intimately by name. . . '

'Yes, yes, get on with it man, what about the wire. . . lots of folk around here drink with pigs, get on with the bit about the wire. Did he strangle himself with it?' demanded a very annoyed coroner, who'd not been so frustrated since he missed his turn with matron at public school. 'Get on with it!'

'Oh, touched a nerve here,' thought Scraghill, wondering if the coroner himself was implicated and ought to be investigated and secondly how long he could drag out his answer about the wire, 'Ah yes, the wire, I'll be coming to that all in good time,' he replied slowly, 'my own,' thought Scraghill with the smile of a man perusing Gulag plans for the English upper classes. 'His, the deceased's, relationship with his porky pals was about to come to an end, his wife had discovered about his drinking soirées and had made plans for Euthan Aziers Abbatoir Services to arrive prematurely. . . for all concerned as it happens. He determined to end it all cleverly so no one would suspect, but he didn't count on such a thorough investigation.'

'Yes, yes, man, get on with it,' twitched the coroner, worried his angina and piles would be aggravated by the tensions this oaf of a Doctor, if indeed he was a real one, was causing him, 'the wire, the wire.'

Miss Hades Vendetter made little personal notes by the side of everything that was said, this was one of the best inquests she'd been on since one of the pub customers bet that he could hang-glide off the cliffs using only a frame tent and some string. Some say he must have made it and flown to Wales, others that he faked it as a jest and was moving house anyway, yet others believed the evidence of an unidentified body found out at sea. *(Not an unusual occurrence during the Exmoor troubles they say.)*

'After plying his friends, I mean his pigs, with enough mature beer slops to drop an Ox or a stoker, and himself on imbibing sufficient anaesthetising quantities of quality local brewed ale, he threw himself into the deep mud of the pig pen, cleverly engaging his foot through the electric fence as he did so. The electric wire kept him safe from the pigs and allowed him to drift off into a peaceful but twitching stupor, eventually the batteries went flat, the pigs, like most blokes after a few beers were hungry and that was that. The only thing left was a booted foot on the outside of the fence, which I presume will find Christian burial at the conclusion of this inquest. I suspect that the landlord will be renewing his customer's acquaintance in the guise of the pub's Sunday roast dinners. My conclusion is guilty of suicide with collusion by his mates the pigs.'

Doctor Remus Blenheim-Landrace Esq OBE, chairman of the local hunt committee and an internationally celebrated Cavy/Wallaby cross breeder, smirked a secret brotherhood smirk as Dr Scraghill was taken away in a straight-jacket, screaming 'you wait till the revolution, you're first against the wall.' This statement was recorded by Miss Hades with glee and used in the psychiatric report, increasing doubt on the good doctor ever being released. The chief psychiatric nurse, R Arfbake OBE RCN, was an old fraternal associate of Dr Remus and had promised to see Scraghill had all the treatment he needed for long term correction. . . apparently they had stored some early electrical equipment in the basement, and it still worked.

'Misadventure,' shouted the coroner, violently whacking the gavel down with an aristocratic relish as if eliminating some commy infiltrator from his version of society.

It was all over, the records were conveniently 'lost' somewhere in the 'files' and the local paper *Moonraker's Weekly*, edited by Mr Bertram 'Snooks' Wilberforce Junior OBE published a brief account of 'hero publican gives life to stop fanatical left wing pigs attacking village'. The Coroner praised the publican who we cannot name for legal reasons and said that 'he would be sadly missed at the meetings and indeed at the pub. . . where you could still always count on a good Sunday dinner.'

So, nobody knows, all except a little old lady called Miss Hades, and now you.

Best not tell, if you know what's good for you. .

**

'The greatest hazard in life is to risk nothing. By not risking you are chained by your certitudes, and are slaves, having forfeited your freedom. Only one who risks is free.' Zen Osho
**

19

Gaylord Simpson. . . milkman

Born Susan Simpson to a reclusive farming family on the moors of Devon, she grew up with a morbid fascination for the breeding habits of the local livestock. Susan was a loner at school and forever longed for the rough and tumble of the boys. They didn't like this as she was blessed with a brutish strength and wanton disregard for suffering – other people's.

Girl's clothing was rejected in favour of more manly clobber and she found a leaning towards the usual pursuits of boys. You know the sort of thing. . . shooting a teddy bear with a BB gun instead of dressing it up and parading it about in a pram. Susan did have a pram for her 12th birthday but by the following week she'd ripped the wheels off it and made a trolley. Her father branched out with a dairy farm and made a successful round in the local community. Susan was given the job of milk delivery. Her father was thrilled how she took to it. Always keen to be started even with rain or frost in the early hours of the morning, and quite often finished before it was light. Customers were always delighted to find fresh milk left in eerie silence on their doorstep before they awoke.

The truth of it was, Susan didn't want to be seen. People would talk to her as though she was a woman. Behind her back those who had seen her lumbering hulk shifting several crates at a time had doubts about that and what they must feed her on back at the farm. Steroids? Hormones? Antibiotics and enzymes? God only knows.

When both her parents died of the rare cattle disease, *bovo en-cryptosis*, Susan inherited the farm and began her experiments in earnest. Her voice was already quite deep, and, by impersonating her deceased father, ordered several state of the art biological growth substances from the Dept of food and fisheries. She was happy in her privacy at the farm and changed her name to Gaylord. She thought it suited her fine. She began an intensive breeding programme with selected cows and formulated the feed stuff herself from various experimental drugs and the odd plant from the Columbian rain forest.

It was all part of a long term plan. She wanted company, her sort of company, and somewhere out there she was going to make it happen. Her first target was a rugged bachelor policeman who lived in an end terrace. Each day a carefully blended mix of special cow juice and hormones was delivered to his door. Six months later she noted the sort of changes of which she could only dream. Sure enough, there were women's clothes hanging on the washing line. He still lived alone and they were his size. It was time to increase the dosage and begin to broaden the experimental group. The whole terrace would become her laboratory. Gaylord had no time for normal life, no TV for him, what with his experimentation and absorbing studies into the sex lives of gay farm animals he was a busy man.

This was all many years ago and you'd think that things will have changed. They have!

Now in his seventies, Gaylord still runs the old family farm but doesn't need to deliver by night, for he now seems the normal one, the whole terrace being a haven for all manner of biologically altered variations of human was-beings. Look around you. Who has milk in their tea? Do their clothes seem odd? Fit properly? Have their voices changed lately or their appetite increased? Does their Christian name ring true? Do they eat too many biscuits for their gender?

Me? I don't drink milk, not any more.

**

'The feelings we feel are created by the thoughts we think.'

**

20

Who saved the fireman?

This is a true tale, told me by a fellow fireman of a real incident he attended. We'll call him Bill, for that was his name. He was a highly experienced and worthy firefighter who had transferred from another brigade. In his time he had experienced tragedies of the worst kind, however, this was not one of them.

I shall paraphrase Bill's words.

'It was an old, fairly large building, plenty of timber in its construction and it was used as a Spiritualist Church. Probably three fire engines in attendance, perhaps more. The fire was intense and severe, my colleague and I, wearing breathing apparatus and carrying a branch and hose, made our way along a ground floor corridor to tackle the fire. There were a number of doors along the corridor accessing individual meeting rooms, the smoke was thick, hot, and the flames were licking along the ceiling. As we quenched the flames we began to turn our attention to the doors off the corridor, there was one we could not open, try as we might, and even if it was locked we should have been able to break it in. It was impossible, believe me, we tried.

Later on, when the fire was finally dead, we went back into the building to inspect. We came to the door we could not open, tried the handle and it opened with ease... but we had to step back sharply, for beyond the doorway was no floor – it had been burned away. Had we opened it during the height of the fire it is quite likely we would have fell into the deep and burning pit to our deaths.

We will never know what held that door shut that fateful night but we will always wonder. And be grateful.'

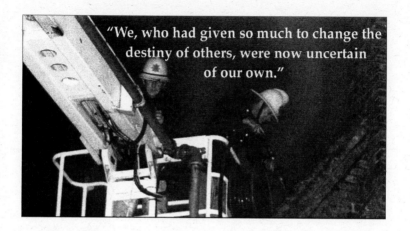

"We, who had given so much to change the destiny of others, were now uncertain of our own."

**

'No argument is so convincing as the evidence of your own eyes.'
**

21

The Piano and the Fire Alarm.

I doubt you'll ever really understand the depth of feeling behind this photo, for the same reason that we cannot listen to music through someone else's ears.

The place is the operational fire training building, Huntingdon, which included furniture and an old piano donated by a good colleague, Dave Hobday. Dave is no longer with us, nor has been for many years now but his memory lives on. One winter's evening, I am alone in the darkened concrete structure, the big fire of wooden pallets is ready to light. This is my last time in a building in which I had worked for many years training fire-fighters in the use of breathing apparatus under realistic conditions. It was an extremely poignant moment for me. Though about to leave the service, my sense of duty drove my diligence. As I waited in the dark I had a mind to keep a memory and set up a camera. (Obviously not very well as it missed out some relevant parts of the scene!)

**

As I typed the above some 15 years later into a blog, the smoke alarm in my house went off; I stopped typing to go and check. There was no reason for the alarm, which had sounded only briefly. It had never done this before and I would add, never since. Perhaps it was Dave's spirit just letting me know he's still about, or perhaps someone else, just letting me know that there is still some connection. Most odd but my fears are allayed by thinking so.

**

As I waited alone, I wandered the training building checking that all was safe and ready for the retained fire crews that would be attending. I lifted the lid of the piano that by now had seen much better days, and played a few notes. I had more skill in moving pianos than playing them though I must say.

I'd set the camera up on timer so couldn't make a nice pose, however, it is a reminder of the passing of many things, life, time, friendships, duty, and sadness too. I suspect music for my ears only, just as it can only ever be.

Revisiting this blog has made me wonder; perhaps my own mind had revisited the psychological state I was in that final night. Perhaps it was that which opened a way for the alarm to sound. Coincidence? Just chance? Perhaps, but you wouldn't ever place a bet on that. . . once in 15 years for a few seconds only and at the very moment I mentioned Dave's name.

**

'The most beautiful experience we can have is the mysterious.
It is the fundamental emotion which stands at the cradle of
true art and true science.' Albert Einstein
**

22

Restored from the dead.
The restoration of a derelict classic sports car.

Would he tell, or wouldn't he? Would he buy, or wouldn't he? Unfortunately for Roy, the answers were pre-ordained. But could he afford to upset his wife again? Only a few months earlier, much to her annoyance, Roy had bought yet another *bargain* wreck to fiddle with in his garage.

She'd told him then, 'Don't you think enough is enough Roy? This one is worse than all the others; for a start, it looks like half of it is missing. Time you gave it up and retired.'

Trouble is, renovating classic cars was in Roy's blood, he doubted he could ever stop, not till they carried him off in a box because God needed a mechanic.

That evening Roy sat quietly with his after dinner cup of tea and thought on how he could tell his wife that he'd recently found the bargain of a lifetime only a couple of streets from where they lived. He must have it. It was in a bit of a mess mind you and the previous owner had died while trying to restore it after a number of years. It was a low mileage, all original, gold, Austin Healey 3000 and the previous owner's unhappy widow just wanted rid of it. 'Bane of my life it was,' she'd said, 'damn thing. His life and soul went into that heap of rubbish. Never saw him until meal times.'

Without consulting his wife, Roy had already agreed to remove it immediately from the premises, along with all the spare parts.

'You can take the tools too, they are no use to me,' she shouted as Roy loaded the trailer. 'Every time I look at them I see him standing there.' Perhaps he'd tell his own wife later, much later, when he'd improved it a bit and she'd forgotten about the other cars he was working on.

He could hardly contain himself. What a bargain it was! He couldn't lose; when finished off properly and to the right buyer, it may well fetch ten times what he'd paid.

For three busy months he never said a word but his wife was more observant than he suspected. She had noticed his habits changing – just like they did every time he had a new project. Signing for several new parts delivered to the house was also a bit of a give away. He was up to something.

Meanwhile, hour by hour, day by day and week by week, Roy toiled ceaselessly on his new pride and joy. To Roy this rusting hulk with more holes than metal was perfect. He didn't see the faults. He only saw this pristine beauty on a country road in sunshine, paintwork and chrome gleaming, the wire wheels spinning through loose gravel to the roar of a three litre engine in its prime and the musical crackle of exhaust on the overrun. Piece by piece the old car was dismantled, cleaned, repainted, bits welded, bits replaced. Roy was oblivious to the fatigue of labour such was his whole being wrapped up in the project. Sometimes a visitor would join him for a chat and a cup of tea but in any event, this particular restoration had never left him feeling alone. In the end, as Roy seemed happy enough, his wife decided to say nothing. Roy would tell her no doubt when he thought he could. It would be two long years before he did.

'I need your help,' he said after dinner one evening.

'What's that then?' she asked. 'Need me to register and insure your new car?'

Roy looked bemused, but smiled, 'How did you guess?'

'I know you of old,' she said, 'you know it will take three weeks to come through, don't you?'

Roy was happy with this, timing was perfect, just a bit of upholstery to finish, put the bonnet back on, fit a new battery and do a last check of nuts and bolts.

'Three weeks will be perfect,' he said. 'Then I've got something special to show you.'

He smiled to himself. When his wife sees his beautifully restored convertible sports car, how could she possibly be cross? Then he could look for another one.

Three weeks later, the car was road legal and ready for a proper test drive. 'I'll show you the new car this morning,' said Roy with pride. He was just itching to get behind the wheel and show it off to the world.

'Not this morning, Roy. I must go shopping first. Perhaps later,' she replied. Cars had never held any fascination for her.

Later that morning and despite being on his own, he gave it a whole hour's test drive just for the sheer pleasure of it, then called home for lunch. 'Are you coming up to the garage and see the new car this afternoon? Goes like a dream - makes you feel alive again.'

'No need Roy, I saw you in it earlier going up and down the road by the shops. It looks nice, pretty cream colour. By the way, who was the old chap smiling and waving to everyone from the passenger seat?'

**

'Our path is but a day we tread,
a gentle walk among possibilities'
Kent Nerburn

**

23

Jessica's Day

'This won't be much fun,' thought Jessica, as she opened the door to another new day. A day heralded by a light grey, rush- hour drizzle.

It was a indeed a new day and a new beginning, in fact just lately for Jessica it had seemed like every new day was a new life in itself. Jessica, a not unattractive lady in her late forties, had just moved to this address, her belongings having passed through that fine doorway only the day before. Her husband was to arrive later. . . he'd stayed overnight at the old place to search for some misplaced documents in the loft, or was it the shed. . . or perhaps the garage. He had recently worked for the railway terminus *lost and found department* but had developed an unfortunate habit i.e. his self-designed filing system was losing that which others had found. In consequence the lost and found job he'd found, was lost. Jessica though had saved the day, she'd found a new job and today was to be her very first with the new organisation - some sort of quasi government venture it was, at least that's the impression she had partially retained.

Jessica stood thinking a moment on the steps outside her fine new front door, a symbolic portal leading to a dream 'Nirvana'. She had dressed comfortably in a smart powder blue loose fitting jacket and skirt complete with matching handbag and shoes. It all seemed so new to her, a new house, and new kitchen, complete with a novel gas powered grill that presented Jessica with an early opportunity to check the efficiency of her new smoke alarms. While she rescued the toast, the abandoned hot tap emptied the hot water tank's contents down the plughole of the kitchen sink from whence it warmed some obscure Victorian sewer at her expense. After scraping the burnt stuff off the toast and a quick wash in cold water Jessica stood in the fine drizzle ready for her day. 'Better take a brolly today... my blue one...' she thought - a thought that coincided with the faint but distinct metallic 'click' from a Yale lock as the door to Nirvana closed unrelentingly behind her.

Jessica patted her jacket pocket for the keys and, despite having clearly felt that the pockets were empty, persisted with a thorough internal check, a search that would have done a pedantic customs officer proud. Next she unbuckled her soft blue leather handbag and rummaged the inner sanctum for the door key. Jessica moved the contents of the bag from one side to the other and back again, luckily it was a light bag with little in it, just the usual stuff, pens, some not having worked for years, last year's diary, phone, tissues, loose change, sweets, purse, various old tickets and receipts, a shopping trolley token, some toiletries, lip balm and hair brush... unluckily, no keys.

At last she could see them, it wasn't so difficult after all, by half squatting on the top step and straining her dominant hand to hold open the highly sprung letterbox she could see her keys quite clearly looking back at her from the hall table... out of reach to all but experienced burglars. With luck Hubby would be there later in the day with spare keys but, for the moment, Jessica's new job called insistently to her from the other side of town, brolly or not, keys or not.

Jessica set off down the street at a good pace, she did not wish to be late and she couldn't remember if it was a nine o'clock start... or maybe it could have been later... or, even, earlier. 'Never mind', she thought, 'I'll get there as early as possible to be sure.' The street was busy with other pedestrians about their day, Jessica became aware that some were staring at her, or at least so she thought. As she walked by a shop window she took the opportunity to glance at her reflection, adjusted her hair and turned her head to one side to see how it looked from a different angle. 'Looks Okay dear,' she said comfortingly to herself as her walk continued. . . accompanied by an even stronger feeling that she was being watched. Luck at last smiled on Jessica, the 40A double-decker bus she needed was just about to leave the stop, when an observant and surprisingly kind conductor waited for her to step aboard. Jessica chose to take the top deck so as to have a better view on life, plus the windows were cleaner. The conductor closely followed her up. She smiled and thanked him as she paid her fare. The conductor fondled her hand as he returned the ticket and change, it gave her the shivers and she noted that the conductor had a seemingly unseemly interest in watching her from under the camouflage of his peaked cap. Jessica shivered again then felt that the seat she was on was either a little cold or perhaps damp so she moved seats, it also meant that she couldn't see the conductor anymore. Jessica stared out of the window at the passing traffic, houses and shops, she was lost deep in thought about the weird day she was having; she couldn't recall having a day like this ever before, none that came to mind. Mind you, recall wasn't one of her specialities.

'Bus terminates here - all change here,' shouted the bus conductor from the stairwell, 'all change here, thank you.' The shout jolted Jessica from her day dream, 'Oh God, no,' her brain screamed at her, 'you've missed your stop. . . you're going to be late.' Jessica brushed past the conductor who almost seemed reluctant to let her by, once her feet were on the pavement she walked briskly, almost militarily, in the direction of her new job, the conductor's eyes followed her, along with her hopes that the job would still be there when she was. 'This is no fun at all,' she thought as she stormed through the rush hour crowds in a state of near panic, the only blessing of which was that she no longer felt the staring eyes of others. At last her new employer's building was in sight, she checked her watch, it read 9.36 am She knew this was probably late but needed to walk slower to gain composure. It wouldn't do turning up on the first day looking like a failed marathon runner, 'first impressions count, stay calm and in control, you look fine, it will be fun,' she told herself. Unfortunately herself was a bad listener and it wasn't long before her breathless hand was on the door handle and unable to pull it open. . . 'I must be really late,' she thought, as through the glass she saw the doorman approach and reach out to unlock the door. . . but he didn't, he merely pulled the door inwards and pointed politely to a little sign on the outside that *Push'*.

'Oh, dear, I'm so sorry,' apologised Jessica as she hurried along with her embarrassment to the reception desk. The doorman said nothing but his eyes followed her with bemused interest.

'I'm Jessica,' she said, 'I'm sorry I'm late and I'm afraid I've forgotten your name too, sorry.'

The receptionist, Tracey, smiled and said, 'Don't worry, we're quite used to that here, it's our department's version of normality,' and smiled again as she paged for her boss.

Soon a little old lady arrived from a back office. She was short with a slight stoop and looked up at Jessica, her eyes peering out from the space between the top of her spectacles and her light brown permed hair. 'Lovely to meet you dear, Josie isn't it?' she enquired. Jessica corrected her but the little old lady didn't seem to notice and continued, 'This way Josie, I'll show you to your office, you have one all to yourself which you'll later share with your own dedicated staff.' So saying, the old lady led the way along a plush carpeted corridor to a large smartly painted wooden door on which a piece of paper in scribbled handwriting declared, *'Jesicka's Office"*.

She opened the door. 'Oh, how lovely,' smiled Jessica, 'oh, what a beautiful desk and that chair. . . oh, and a window with a view on the world, lovely, just lovely.' It was going to be a fun day after all. As the old lady left the room she stopped and turned using her whole body to do so and said, 'Your greeting pack to the organisation is on your desk dear, if you need anything else ask that girl Josie at reception, okay?'

Jessica sat in that fine soft chair; it felt a lot warmer than that bus seat for sure. She slid the greetings file across the leather topped desk and began to read the front cover. . . Greeting Pack for Jessica (*surname withheld; data protection act*), Head of Research and Promotion for the Department of Social Health for the Elderly; The Alzheimer Awareness Project.

Dawn rose slowly in the recesses of her mind and she remembered what job it was for which she'd interviewed. The door was knocked softly then opened a little, the little old lady's head peeked around the opening. . . 'Excuse me for interrupting you dear but the doorman thought I really ought to say something to you. . . did you know you've got the back of your skirt tucked into your knickers. . . all right dear?'

**

*'One eye on the destination means
only one eye on the path.'*
**

24

Dichotomy of a Brotherhood Bargain.

Nathan Sykes hunched his shoulders and stared thoughtfully into an empty beer glass in the *'Live and Let Live'* Inn, a spit and sawdust meeting place for the rough and ready lower classes. Big Jack Tyler, swarthy and rugged landlord, looked like he was born to run such a cut-throat establishment. 'So Nathan, you been away on holiday these last six months then? Butlin's or her Majesty's place? '

'Rather not say, Tyler my friend. I been dealt some bad cards in life. I deserved better you know. Skilled bricklayer me, but you got to know the right people to get the right job. I tried for the Masonic club for years so I could make the right contacts but they turned me away.'

'Well Nathan, if you're still interested, see that chap in the corner over there?' Tyler points to a dark corner of the pub. 'He's one of them funny hand-shake blokes. He might help. He's always alone, never seen him buy a drink yet neither.'

Nathan stared into the darkness, seeing no one. When he looked a second time, he could just make out a tall gentleman, smartly dressed with a long black coat. He decided he would give them one more try, after all, what had he to lose? 'Evening sir, may I join you?'

The gentleman, who had the appearance of an undertaker, nodded and gestured with his hand.

Nathan took notice of the hand movement, just in case it was one of the secrets he needed later. 'Is that a secret gesture sir?' he inquired with a smile, he was a cheeky rogue, despite a truly merciless criminal past.

'No, I'm merely pointing to the chair. But I guess from your question I might surmise the purpose of your attention. If you have a wish to join the brotherhood, then sit and tell me about yourself.'

Nathan spent the next hour selectively confessing his crimes and making excuses for previous rejections. Finally pleading for one more chance – in return for which there was *nothing* he wasn't prepared to do.

The old gentleman made a gesture with his left hand and said, 'You may be in luck, one of the brothers has, er, moved on. You seem like just the one to take his place. Be here tomorrow night at the same time and I will take you to the desired place. Do not be late. Do not tell a soul.' He reached out a hand, which Nathan took eagerly, studying every nuance of the grip. For who knows what is secret and what is not? The gentleman's hand was icy cold, 'Gor Blimey,' thought Nathan. 'That's what comes of sitting in a dark corner too long.' But he was too excited to think more on it. He must go home – no more robberies for him – he would be rich once he was in with that lot. Easy jobs, easy money. Once he was in, he'd show 'em, he'd teach them a lesson for rejecting him too. He put on a kindly voice, 'Goodnight to you sir. Good night Tyler!'

Next day, Nathan Sykes was a new man, something had changed in him.

'God - if ever there was one,' he thought, 'has brought hope at last.' However, it was not to God but to Tyler the landlord, he offered up thanks. He would always be indebted to him. Though he might not drink there any more; not once he was a brother. As he walked through town, past St Paul's Church and into the busy market square by the river, he met a couple of the men he had begged for help in the years before, he smiled and nodded to them, gesturing with his hand like the gentleman had – just in case it was a sign. They smiled back and nodded too. Nathan spent a good hour in the sunshine amongst the market people, nodding, smiling and gesturing. Perhaps it was all as simple as that. . . he looked forward with increasing relish to knowing more secrets.

The appointed hour was close and darkness fell stealthily upon the town. Nathan had arrived early at the 'Live and let Live' to fortify his nerves with a few beers. The old gent eventually appeared in the shadows of a side door and silently beckoned Nathan to join him. Soon they were hurrying along the pitiless, narrow terraced streets towards the lane by the river, where the lodge had stood for some two hundred years. Nathan had many questions but it was as much as he could do to keep up with the old man, who obviously wasn't in a talkative mood this time.

At the lodge entrance, the old gent explained to Nathan that this would be a turning point in his life. Now he must choose, either to go forward or return to whence he came. Whatever his choice, it was final, there being no second chance.

Nathan wasn't completely stupid, he reckoned this was merely one of the first tests. Well, he'd show them. 'Forward. It's time I had what I deserve. I'm ready.'

The old gent slowly rapped three times on the door, watched carefully by Nathan, who was absorbing all the secrets he could.

The door opened into a small vestibule with bare boarded floor and coat racks with a dozen or so old-fashioned cloaks and coats. The gent's cold hand on his back ushered Nathan inside. The door closed behind them and they were in darkness. When you've burgled a few homes, darkness is something you become used to but Nathan had to dig deep to overcome a sense of foreboding. This was different.

The old gent spoke: 'May the light of those gone before, now shine.'

A weird glow appeared in the room, just enough to make out two figures, the gent and now one other, as though spirited in from nowhere. Desperate not to forget any of the secrets, especially this clever one on - how to turn on the lights - Nathan was so intent on mentally repeating the words over and again, he hardly noticed the preparations for his initiation. He was past caring anyway, he didn't mind what happened as long as he learned the secrets to the life he desired, and so richly deserved.

The gent spoke again, 'Nathan Sykes, with the power invested in me by those who went before, I will now lead you into the lodge to meet your fate. My advice is simple. Keep to the rules and obey all requests, no matter how strange they seem. You will be blindfolded throughout; this is for *your* protection. I now advise you most strongly, do not cheat, do not try to see. If you do, well. . . I'll leave it at that. You have been warned. You made your decision outside these doors. Now, you can only make the best of it.'

Nathan began to speak but was interrupted by a hand across his mouth, 'You will not speak out of turn, not where *you* are going. Stay silent. Do not worry. I will be here at the end to lead you back into town.'

It felt to Nathan that the ceremony went on for hours. He'd been led in and around what seemed like catacombs. Once, led down a spiral stairwell, the air had turned earthy, there was the damp smell of old lime. Someone had tried to disguise it with herb incense, but he'd been a bricklayer too long to be fooled by that. All manner of visions came to him as his mind compensated for loss of sight. He was filled with a sense that something was dead or dying in the surrounding blackness. Finally, the ceremony with all its rituals came to an end and he was accepted as one of them. Still in darkness, and not once had he dared test the old gent's words about cheating, each of the brothers offered up the secret grip, always exactly the same way and all of them with cold hands. Nathan thought that the place needed heating, all hanging about in the dark like that, no wonder they were cold. Once he'd been a few times he would suggest a fire of some sort, yes, that would do, what they needed was a jolly good fire.

Thrilled with the night's proceedings and clutching as many secrets as he could carry in his head, Nathan was led back into town by the old gent. It was late, street lamps were few and far between, and a night mist had risen from the river. The old gent shook Nathan's trembling hand, Nathan responded as best he could. 'Remember,' said the old gent, 'there is no going back for you now, you are one of us. I will come and find you when it is time.'

Nathan shuddered at the gent's bony and icy grip and the tone of his words but put it down to damp night air.

'Thank you sir for opening the door for me. I look forward to your calling. Good night.'

Next day Nathan Sykes, newly born of the brotherhood, stepped into early morning sunshine and set off to the market place to try out his new secrets. He was in luck, one of the gentlemen he'd met the other day was approaching. Nathan smiled, nodded and held out his hand, quietly uttering a password. The man responded in kind and asked when and where Nathan had joined the fraternity. Nathan was over the moon. . . it worked. From now on everything was going to be different, oh, so different. 'Why, brother, were you not there last night at the lodge by the river? That was me being led around in the dark.'

Nathan paused as a puzzled expression spread over the man's face. He looked uneasy, even shocked.

'But brother Sykes, we have our new lodge now, behind the library in Harpur Street. The old one burned down, as it happens, six months ago to the day. To be honest we only ever felt comfortable in numbers there, few could tolerate being alone. After the fire, the building was demolished and during excavations a number of bodies were found. They're still investigating of course, possibly an old plague pit but to tell the truth it's still a mystery. So, all joking aside, where did you join?'

Nathan had no time for further talk. He was on his way to the 'Live and Let Live'. There were questions needing answers.

Nathan Sykes was last seen late that same evening, walking quickly in the gathering darkness towards the lane by the river. A lamp-lighter on his rounds reported that Mr Sykes looked agitated and seemed to be talking to himself, for there was no other with him.

The 'Live and Let Live' was demolished to make way for the modern bus station that stands there today. The Lodge in its new home prospered more than ever. The building was a pleasure to enjoy in solitude and contemplation.

This strange tale of Nathan Sykes comes to us from the diary of the late Reverend Robert J Williams, incumbent of St Paul's Parish 1951 – 1958 and the last brother Nathan was ever to meet in the light of day

**

'Men occasionally stumble over the truth,
but most of them pick themselves up and
hurry off as if nothing has happened.'

Winston Churchill.

**

25

Your Government needs you.
(A one way street - allegedly)

This work of fiction is not based on any persons living or dead and bears no resemblance either to the Government of the day or any British Broadcasting Corporation, past or present.

High up in a plush, pent house office suite of Broadcaster House, something rather more foul than normal was about to come home to roost.

'It's the Home Secretary on the line for you Sir Hugh, he insists that it is most urgent and highly confidential,' explained Ms Bo, Sir Hugh's long overlooked and undervalued Personal Assistant.

'Put him through Ms Bo,' replied the totally unqualified Executive-in-Chief Sir Hugh 'Peregrine' Braggington Havalot as he turned the volume down on his games console. He'd been blessed with inheriting the post when his step cousin, Lord Willy Hademdown the third, an unplanned product of selective inbreeding, died unexpectedly suddenly at a weekend grouse shoot on his boyfriend's 'not for profit' country estate.

Sir Hugh had earned the nick name 'Peregrine' due to his accent, purportedly aristocratic background and the elevated position of his office from which he surveyed his prey far down below in the bustling metropolis. He knew nothing of this and to be honest, he knew nothing of very much at all.

The primly dressed, sixty year old Ms Bo, Boedica Flabergast, on the other hand was eminently qualified but had been actively ignored for any further promotion. Basically she was too clever and always posed a potential threat to the dim witted who had normally found their own promotion surprisingly easy. Despite having unstintingly worked her little ice-blue cotton socks off for over forty years at the Corporation, she was now fated to work until sixty seven before even being entitled to a pension. She had seen many a senior executive retire much younger on various and nefarious grounds, usually incompetence, and still receive an impressive life pension and a mind boggling golden handshake. Something, along with the entire working popula-tion of the country, she could never fathom. Failure seemed to have its own peculiar rewards.

Oh, they had fobbed her off with their plausible excuses - when she was young and enthusiastic they needed someone more experienced, more mature - when she was older and more experienced they decided they needed someone younger, some-one more daring, not institutionalised.

'Institutionalised?' To Boedica's keenly observant mind most of the senior staff at the Corporation should be sectioned and living in an institution and they soon would be too, if she ever had her way.

'Ah, Hugh, old boy,' came the Home Secretary's plum in the mouth Etonian voice, 'just thought I'd let you know about a new super bonus scheme we are pushing through the lobbies to ad-vantage our finest and most loyal public servants such as your good self. Just thought I'd keep you in the loop for old time's sake, you know. Well that's it old boy, you must come to dinner some time, bring the little woman if she insists. . . . Oh, I almost forgot, we need you to do the Government a small favour, keep us out of the news for a day or two. . . find something else, something exciting that doesn't mention the government at all, almost like we are on a different planet.'

Boedica controlled a snort and silently concurred that the Government might as well be on another planet for all the good they did. She then gently, with a skill that can only come with extensive practice, replaced the receiver. Forty years working among the gaily self-centred cunning of senior executives had taught her a good few tricks and her pension would be gra-ciously enhanced by the sale of her memoirs, an exposé of the inept, corrupt and insane that ruled the country over four decades.

Sir Hugh slowly replaced the receiver, deep in thought about the important information that had just been shared with him and possibly him alone by the illustrious Home Secretary himself. . . bonuses eh? Super bonuses! Then he remembered that there was something else the Home Secretary had mentioned – ah yes, a good news story with no Government interference. . . or was it no Government mention? No matter, Sir Hugh was a very powerful man, even if short of a full set of working neurons he had handfuls of old school chums who still maintained influential positions in the establishment and often in no small measure due to Sir Hugh's continuing mutual discretion.

As he pictured himself draped in plush ermine and dozing peacefully in the cosy ambience of the House of Lords, he pondered on the possibilities of the Government's dilemma. . . the one on which they didn't want any publicity.

'What could it be?' he wondered, mentally thumbing through a long list of as yet unpublicised possibilities, 'perhaps the clerical error that resulted in the long overdue and over budget new aircraft carrier being named 'HMS Hopeless'?. . . or the old boy's network think tank pontificating on making being gay compulsory ?. . . or worse still, having sold off the people's coal, oil, gas, water, forests, electricity, steel, fishing quotas and fracking rights under people's homes to foreign powers, (in order to fund foreign aid schemes and keep the USA congress contented by buying Trident), perhaps it was the latest draft treasury plans to tax the air we breathe. It would be funded by private finance initiatives and allow for generous shareholder dividends. There would be exceptions naturally. . . the dead of course, pensioners and people in comas would be on reduced rates while athletes and the like (the obese of the air breathing population) would pay a premium super rate. Mmm, could be any one of numerous faux pas,' muttered Sir Hugh as he picked up the telephone. As he lifted the receiver to his one good ear he heard a slight noise, 'must get this phone looked at, always get a clicking on it, could be MI5,' he mumbled.

Ms Bo knew better!

'Get me Genghis, the news desk editor at once Ms Bo,' he snapped without even the faintest pretence of politeness. Politeness wasn't something he needed in his high social circles where, like buzzards, they were immune from the riffraff far below. Sir Hugh's old school house tie, Buzzard House he was in, featured circling buzzards over an injured Wildebeest, symbolic of aspiring beyond the working class masses, waiting until they are too weak to fight back.

'Please note that Genghis is only an inter departmental nickname Sir Hugh, you want David Carn. . . I'll put you through straight away,' thinking how popular her memoirs will eventually be with an entire assortment of people from named executives to unknown riff-raff, she smiled the smile she would have had long ago had life and the Corporation been more kind to her.

'Ah good, Carn, drop everything, put a hold on anything currently newsworthy about the Government and get yourself up here to my office. . . now!' Sir Hugh had made a start, he put his games console in his desk drawer and stared at his office door impatiently, 'where was that idiot Carn?'

A cautious knock heralded the arrival of one David 'Genghis' Carn, a man sharing absolutely no characteristics with his namesake, a nervous twitchy sop like man whose indiscretions in the news room had been instrumental in his rapid promotion beyond his level of competence. Knowledge of his sexual adventures with various vegetables in the Corporation's staff canteen commanded total loyalty from him, whatever the task he was set. A big mortgage, his wife being a psychiatrist and the fear of some unpleasant years in a specially selected prison saw to that.

'Come on in Carn, come in, sit down and listen carefully,' shouted Sir Hugh, he'd never liked Carn. . . he'd gone to a state school like had that awful Bo woman. Sir Hugh was of the opinion that such factory fodder should never be trusted and must always be kept in their place.

Genghis sat timidly, crossing his legs, staring at Sir Hugh's vast empty desk top and fumbled with his fingers. 'Right, Carn, got a job for you, we need to run a great news story over the next few days that doesn't mention politicians or the government of the day. . . got it? said Sir Hugh, leaning forward and wiping little bits of talking spit off his highly polished Amazonian hardwood desk. He was fond of his desk, not likely to get another like this one. . . it being made from illegally sourced and virtually extinct timber.

'Th..th.. there's nothing m..m..much happening I'm afraid,' stammered a terrified Genghis, he'd never liked Sir Hugh and had a great distrust of any one who didn't go to a proper school, a state school. God alone knows what went on in those hoity toity private establishments, and even God can't bear to look. Genghis feared being drawn into the Public school elite circles. . . his wife's tales of Public school related clients were enough to make him keep his distance. . . they weren't the sort of friends he wanted. 'What about something foreign? A sex scandal? Bank corruption?' continued Genghis.

Sir Hugh's white knuckled fist thumped the desk, 'I told you dopey, nothing to do with the Government. What's wrong with you man?' snarled the man in charge of the country's impartial face of freedom of the press. 'I have a plan of my own. . . the weather. People like to hear about the weather. Make it a snow storm on its way. Get that incompetent weather bloke out of retirement and get him to tell the people about an impending Arctic storm that will paralyse the country. Do a news item on looking after the frail and buying in food while they still can. One day we do the warning, the next day we do the weather and on the third day we apologise. It won't be our fault; we'll blame the environment agency and the Met office, plus initiating a grand public sacking of the idiot weather man. There you are, easy, all sorted. . . now get on with it.'

'B..b..but Sir Hugh, the weather is fine, the only snow is in Scotland, some remote village somewhere in the Craggygorms or something. . . ' stuttered a confused Genghis. Even he knew this was a daft idea.

'You leave the met office and the EA to me; you'll soon have enough storm warnings to wallpaper the building. Get that pretty blonde reporter to go to where ever that snow is, you know the one I mean, the bimbo with the big boobs, everybody likes her. Send her with a select team in the Corporation Helicopter immediately and explain that her entire career depends on making this look like an ice age Armageddon. Go!'

His plan beginning to take shape and a couple of e-mails later to contacts in the departments that would make it work, Sir Hugh reached for his calculator and began to work out his expenses for when he became a Lord. As he pondered over the cost of duck houses and business lunches in the Seychelles, the phone rang. It was that fool Genghis again, though Ms Bo always introduced him by his proper name and title, 'Yes, what is it now Carn,' snapped an impatient Sir Hugh as he watched his calculator time out and fade.

'It's the hell..hell..helicopter Sir Hugh. It's r..r..run out of airworthy service time, if you remember we c..c..cut its budget to allow for a bigger party this Christmas,' explained a reluctant David 'Genghis' Carn, listening intensely for the shot that would kill the messenger.

'Right, get this Carn and get it good. Tell the bloody pilot if he ever wants to work again then he's to fly the bloody thing to Scotland - tell him that! If the bloody thing crashes all the better, we'll have a better story than a bit of isolated snow: 'Pretty, pregnant, single young reporter on drugs dies while running away with perverted drunken pilot in stolen helicopter etc'. . . but don't tell him *that* bit, dopey!' Sir Hugh slammed down the receiver and tried to retrieve his expenses data from the calculator.

Ms Boadica Flabbergast winced and held her ear as she slowly replaced the receiver. . . this was wonderful stuff, she could see chapter eleven of her book being read by Sir Hugh himself. . . as he served out at least ten years at her majesty's pleasure.

Meanwhile, somewhere deep in the Craggygorms at the little snowbound village of Glen Invergrumpy, the post lady was conveying a telegram to the sheep farmer who ran the airfield.

'Better move they sheep off the runway McTaggart, they'll no be long frae London by helicopter,' she advised.

McTaggart called into one of his barns where he allowed several East Europeans to live, in return for various labours and favours. . . they were a lot cheaper than locals for sure. Handing out shovels and with some hand signals of his own invention he soon had them clearing snow from the runway. A lot of it was swept into the cattle grid half way along the airstrip, 'It'll take the bumps out of it for sure,' he thought, as he and his dog Wallace, a huge Rotweiller-Collie cross, (cross being a habitually operative word) drove the nervous and unbranded sheep into the worker's barn, 'save heating that, them sheep'll keep 'em warm for sure.' Wallace was fully trained, in what exactly we may never know but an English accent would trigger his hackles to rise and lips curl back in a terrifying display of well used bone crushers. He wasn't called Wallace for nothing.

The Corporation 'select' team consisted of Rob 'mad marine' Oakes, whose time in the SAS had seen him fly helicopters with a lot less than some silly airworthiness certificate; pretty blonde Samantha Wilfershore the sex symbol of the Corporation and who had created more unusable out-takes from interviews than any one else in history; Nigel Yorner, a forty something divorcee from Cornwall on sound. . . and a fair variety of anti depressants; finally young and spotty Skunk 'Spielberg' Harrison, the only cameraman willing to join the expedition and who had inherited a wild sense of adventure from his commune parents.
. . that and a mild and intermittent dose of schizophrenia.

McTaggart had only just cleared his 'volunteers' off the runway and out of sight in their barn when the helicopter skimmed snow off the nearby hill and swept engine screaming into the valley at just over thistle height, Rob's eyes were open wide with excitement as he relived an attack on a mountain outpost he'd been somewhere in the world. . . he was never quite sure where it was, at one time he thought it might have been Wales. As he slewed the chopper into what looked like a hand brake turn and a dead stop the contents of the helicopter were thrown to one side. . . eyes all firmly closed with fear.

Before the rotors had stopped turning, Rob 'mad marine' Oakes had his platoon disembarked and running to the field perimeter complete with what little baggage they had for an over nighter. McTaggart directed them to his garden shed which doubled as the airfield customs and immigration terminal.

'Papers please,' he asked, holding out his hand, which received an arctic stare from Rob and a warm and pretty handshake from Samantha, 'Oh well, never mind the papers, we can always do that silly stuff later,' said the now grinning and newly besotted McTaggart. Skunk gave him a suspicious look but still managed to get a few frames shot. . . you never know when the ordinary will become the extra ordinary. *'Be prepared'* had been his motto ever since being thrown out of the boy scouts for selling naughty photos to his pals.

'You'll no doubt all be booked in at the village pub, just down the lane about half a mile. You can't miss it, it has an embalmed stuffed sheep for a swinging sign by the car park. . . it's called the Merry Shepherd, lovely place, peat fire, great whiskey. . . home grown as they say. . . nod nod. . . May see more of you in there later,' said McTaggart, still reluctant to take his eyes off Samantha.

Rob was already on his second pint when they joined him in the bar.

The landlady was also a McTaggart, second cousin by marriage it was alleged, a fine, burly but secretive woman who'd at one time held ambitions for the Olympic shot put event but had unfortunately damaged her shoulder in a poaching accident while wrestling a full grown stag to the ground.

Skunk checked his camera, yes, he'd managed a good few frames of the pub and its fearsome landlady. He was pleased with the footage already so far obtained, the crazed eyes of the demoniacal pilot, the staring eyes of McTaggart the airfield controller, the burning, fearsome crushing eyes of the landlady and lots of furtive glimpses of Samantha, 'yes it was going well,' he told his other self, who for a rare change was actually listening.

The team settled in for the night, well fed on lamb stew and potatoes and well plied with spirits courtesy of some anonymous benefactor. Samantha retired early so as to try on her white leather one piece ski suit and practice her lines in front of the mirror, a suspicious looking bit of furniture screwed to the wall of her bedroom. Farmer McTaggart watched with interest from the other side.

The rest of the team were watching the TV and hardly believing what was being said on the news. . . 'Amber alert across the country. . . only essential travel advised. . . check on old people. . . prepare for power failure, etc.' Having flown over the entire country on the way to Glen Invergrumpy and seen not one single snow flake on the way they wondered what on earth was going on.

'Perhaps it's a repeat,' said Nigel, '98% of transmissions are repeats. . . I reckon I've seen 'em all. Anyway that's the weather geezer that got the sack for misinforming the nation about some great storm. Just shows. . . there's some glimmer of hope for all of us,' he concluded in a depressed and without any hope at all voice.

Back in London all was well. The retired weather idiot had been wheeled out and done his stuff. They'd told him it was a documentary about great weather men of the 21st century; that, a free taxi ride, 200 quid cash in hand and a crate of stout was all he needed. He was going to be famous again and didn't he know it!

Sir Hugh had by now made all his necessary important and highly confidential phone calls, including one to the Home Secretary to tell him, 'Whatever it is you never asked me to do has been done. I'll say no more,' at the same time thinking, 'Actually I don't know any more. . . best kept that way I reckon. What you don't know, you can't be blamed for.' He'd also watched climatic Armageddon being prophesied on the main news which was followed by a genuine news flash about riots and food looting in two major cities, fuelled by panic about the impending great storm. Rival channels, fearing they had somehow missed something important, repeated the warnings without any corroborating evidence though still managed to over emphasise blame on the Corporation for causing the riots.

Sir Hugh smirked a Lordly smirk, it was better than he'd anticipated, the news was filled to the brim but without any mention of Government at all, a resounding success. He'd also naively asked Ms Bo to check over his expenses claims which had taken him nearly all afternoon to create. She did check them. . . and then made a photo-copy for herself, 'Appendix Expenses Scandals,' she thought.

They all went to bed that night with a collection of their own dreams. . . none of them shared, Ms Bo was fighting off publishers and paparazzi and Sir Hugh, I mean Lord Hugh of Cambria, was making his maiden speech in a packed house of lords to rapturous applause from all sides. Ah, dreams eh?

It was fine morning that saw a bright Sun shining over the Merry Shepherd Pub and Rob 'mad marine' Oakes checking out the bruises on his arms, trophies from a late night arm wresting competition with the landlady. Skunk had already been busy with his camera, including catching a furtive Farmer McTaggart tip toeing along the landing late last night. Skunk was determined that both of him would make it to the top one day. . . by some means or another, by tenacity, skill and innovation. . . or perhaps, just blackmail. Skunk also had some great infra red night shots of a light aircraft landing at the field and some posh looking geezers with brief cases and what appeared to be gorilla like bodyguards making their way down the lane to a big house at the far end of the village. Skunk never did do much sleeping.

Up at the big house, a large clandestine holiday property owned by the Government and used mainly by members of the cabinet for various deviant pleasures under the auspices of 'Wild Nature Adventures', important discussions were afoot. The Home Secretary himself was there along with the Foreign Secretary, various civil servants, someone's old school chum, a cleaning lady in the basement sleeping off half the drinks cabinet and a few sheep fanciers. They were there to do a private and friendly deal with representatives from an oil rich ex-communist country with whom they were publicly definitely not friendly. It was essential to maintain secrecy, hence the 'request' to the Corporation for non political news and so far all was going well, they were as oblivious to the Corporation team's presence at the Merry Shepherd as the team were to the Government presence at the big house. The foreign representatives were reticent about speaking inside the house, they suspected listening devices and the like. . . the like of which they would have done had the tables been reversed. They insisted upon walking in the dry stone walled grounds of the big house. Anyway, they were used to the cold and took no small pleasure in seeing the port reddened faces of the home diplomats shivering in the weak sunshine.

Meanwhile back at the Merry Shepherd it was breakfast time. As McTaggart the landlady dollopped out great ladles of salted porridge for each of her guests she attracted an admiring glance from Rob the mad marine and an understanding analytical gaze from Nigel who now felt he understood why she was built like she was. Skunk had already finished his bowlful in the time it took Samantha to wipe mirror clean the dirty spoon and peer into it at her reflection. Even in that she still looked alluringly pretty.

'I take it ye'll all be having the Merry Shepherd's big yin,' McTaggart the landlady asked, although it sounded more like a command.

'And what's that when it's at home Ms McTaggart?' asked a curious yet still sensibly cautious Nigel.

McTaggart pointed one of her huge sausage fingers at the menu board where it proclaimed, 'Satisfaction guaranteed with the Merry Shepherd's Big One – full breakfast, 2 lamb chops, 3 bacon rashers, 3 eggs, home made black pudding, chips and beans. £5.95.'

Samantha shuddered a little, count her out of that, she had a figure to watch.

The three men almost instinctively opted for the breakfast and contented themselves with watching someone else's figure. Nigel and Skunk watched Samantha's and Rob watched that fine feminine prop forward figure of a landlady, he'd not seen anyone built like that since stalking Silverbacks in western Africa.

Negotiations were progressing well, back in the chilly gardens of the big house, it wasn't only oil that lubricated, when it came to the wheels of government, money did that. . . usually lots of it and often to be found, or rather not found, in the bulging coffers of some off shore tax haven.

Senior negotiator, Vladimir Krushemovski, known as Vlad the impaler in government circles, walked close to the home secretary, known as the smiling assassin in foreign circles, 'as long as the people do not find out, all will be good. What about your famous investigative newspapers and their teams of illegal hackers? Are we safe?'

The Home Secretary smiled one of his now well publicised and practised smiles, 'they all have their price, they are more interested in making money than truth. We keep them out of prison. . . they keep us out of the papers. They are loyal supporters and share a common dream. . . that of seeing their names in the new years honours list.'

'Crikey ! What the hell . . .' interrupted the Foreign Secretary, grabbing the Home Secretary's shoulder and pointing towards a man about a hundred yards away on the other side of the wall. The intruder was also pointing with something they couldn't quite make out. . . their way.

In a flash the foreign body guards had knocked them all to the ground behind the wall. As they crawled out of sight through mud and goat droppings back to the house they discussed how to deal with the situation. 'I can have MI5 find him and have him sectioned under the mental health act. . . who ever it is he won't ever bother us again,' cursed the Home Secretary, whose only previous experience at crawling had been first as a baby and later when he wanted the cabinet job.

Vladimir calmly, as though it wasn't at all his first experience in such matters, suggested that they let Big Otto deal with him and they would drop the body out of their plane into the sea on their way home. Big Otto's eyes twitched and he felt his pockets for the 9mm. . . or should he perhaps use the bayonet. . . perhaps the garrote? Ah, choices, choices, he loved them all.

Having returned to the house they dried their mud covered knees by the fire and a touch more sanity ruled once more. After all, nobody knew they were here, it was a secret location and the media were already firmly in their pockets, along with their dirty hankies and some small change. They concluded that it was probably only one of the villagers out bird spotting. Yes that was more like it, a lot of fuss over nothing. Documents and bank account details were exchanged and the guests prepared as best they could for departure, phoning ahead to have clean clothes brought out to the plane on their return to the motherland. There was no desire to convey an image that the ambassadors had in any way been on their knees begging.

At the big house, they remained blissfully unaware of the Corporation's news team and talented film crew ensconced just a few hundred yards away in the Merry Shepherd.

The news team made their way back to the airfield where there was still at least a heap of snow, that is, all except Rob who'd stayed behind to help McTaggart the landlady who had promised him a look at her gun, gin trap and old bones collection. Skunk, with his truly amazing skills at special effects and making the camera lie, took some sweeping shots of a blizzard torn valley, then one of Samantha, sweeping along pristine white leather from foot to blue eyes. Samantha did her thing with the over the shoulder smile at the camera and rambled on in her soft seductive voice some inane drivel about snow and imminent Armadillos. No one would notice what she said anyway. While zooming in close for an eye shot, Skunk saw people running in the reflection, this was a money shot as they called it in the trade. This was the stuff that made good cameramen truly great. He would be investigating more when he had the chance.

'That's a wrap for now Sam,' said Skunk, 'how about sound Nigel, okay?'

'Eh? What's that?' asked Nigel, who for a sound man was rarely listening, 'Oh, yeah, lovely, lovely voice, and even got some sheep baaing in the distance makes it really rural.' As if Invergrumpy, one of the most remote places in the country, could be anything but.

'Right, all back to the pub ready for lunch and I'll send the edited copy back to base by satellite,' enthused a very hyper Skunk who not only had exciting plans but wondered if the satellite system actually stretched to the Craggygorms.

The reflection in Sam's eyes of people running had revealed the two cabinet ministers, a couple of civil servants and the foreign visitors making for McTaggart's alien holiday barn. They'd suddenly spotted the camera crew up at the airfield and decided that discretion was the better part of valour and certainly better than Big Otto's plan to eliminate them all, taking their bodies home to his brother's highly profitable organic pig farm.

They hid in the barn, in the quiet and the dark, not knowing much about who or what was in there. It was quiet but for the heavy breathing of nervous sheep and even more nervous illegal immigrants, some of whom thought they recognised Big Otto from wanted posters back home. On finding the coast was clear and covertly slipping Farmer McTaggart, the airfield controller, a wad of notes and a bottle of 80% proof special Vodka they made their way to the plane. Once airborne it slipped unnoticed under the radar and headed east. All had gone so well, a hero's welcome was assured.

Not so long after all this had transpired, Sir Hugh was informed by David Carn that his snow Armageddon feature was ready to roll out on the main mid day news, 'would he like to pop down to the news room to watch it go out?'

'Well done at last Carn, yes, I'm on my way down, if this works out there'll be a little in it for all of us,' smarmed a sneakily happy Sir Hugh, thinking and chuckling at the same time, 'yes, Ermine for me and a couple of years in Parkhurst for you.'

He pushed his games console into the drawer and made his way to the lift.

Sir Hugh, David Carn and the news controllers gathered behind the glass that separated the news reader from outside interference. 'We've called in our top news broadcaster, one of the old school, great voice, very capable, can roll with the punches,' spoke the lead controller, being interrupted by an impatient Sir Hugh, 'yes, yes, just get on with it,' he said curtly, taking a note of the controller's name for the redundancy list he was working on.

The news credits rolled and the camera zoomed in to the steady face of truth and sturdy voice of justice, Damian 'Benedict Arnold' Moronham, 'Welcome to the mid day news. Today our main story is the chaos caused by the snow storms that have swept and paralysed the country.' Damian couldn't hide a slight look of puzzlement on his face, 'what snow', he thought, 'am I being set up here? Is it a, you've been framed sketch?' From this point on Damien's suspicions were going to influence what and how he spoke. 'We sent a news team to cover one of the worst hit areas in the country, the Craggygorms.' Again Damien sensed something not quite right, I mean, where the hell were the Craggygorms when they were at home? 'But first we have some footage shot during last night's riots and food looting caused by a fear of shortages during the storm. Over to our outside broadcast team in one of our major cities.'

There followed a few minutes of burnt-out shops in seemingly snow free streets. The usual diatribe was wheeled out by the various factions of councillors, shopkeepers, police, the odd passer-by and the occasional masked looter with name changed to protect his identity. It was nothing that Damien hadn't heard before, but where was the bloody snow?

Camera light back on Damien, he continued with no small amount of suspicion in his voice, 'Thank you. And now to our main feature with the lovely Samantha out in the snow in the popular tourist resort of Glen Invergrumpy, apparently the airport was only kept open by the heroic efforts of the residents using hand shovels - an amazing story, let's go to the report . . .'

As the footage sent by Skunk 'Spielberg' Harrison began to play, Damien's suspicions grew. If Glen Invergrumpy had an airport and was a tourist destination, then why in all his years had he not heard of it? He decided that he would go along with whatever the programmer wanted and consult legal advice later. . . it could be an earner for him.

'Ah, that's better,' said Sir Hugh turning to the big monitor and seeing a big picture of blizzards and that pretty blonde bimbo woman. He didn't care what she was droning on about, that leather ski suit was a nice touch though. . . then something horrible went inexplicably through his mind, not sure what had caused an image of a sheep hanging from a sign meant, he looked around at several other puzzled faces. It was the first of many semi subliminal messages that Skunk had inserted into the news piece. He had plans to be great one day, both of him. Scenes depicting snow, cattle grids, a helicopter, Samantha's pretty face and various bits of her anatomy dressed in white leather were interspersed with very brief glimpses of other things - Things like men looking over a wall then ducking down, a woman built like a gorilla and wearing a kilt, some mad crazed staring eyes, a grubby looking man that looked like a farmer and more. The images were only fleeting and never on long enough to clearly see who was who.

'What the hell is going on Carn,' snarled a by now fuming Sir Hugh.

Carn snapped some orders at the controllers, who quickly re-wound their own copy and freeze framed the images. 'There's loads of them sir, looks like they run all the way through.'

'Bloody stop the thing man,' screamed Sir Hugh.

'No can do,' replied the bemused controller, 'we use computers to generate the signal, some clever bastard has built in some sort of over ride, we can't do anything but let it run its course then make some comment about technical errors. That's what we normally do.'

Damien had got the picture in more ways than one and began distancing himself from the report, despite the intermittent begging and threatening that was raging in his earpiece, 'We appear to be experiencing technical interference beyond our control.'

The report continued, transmitting to the nation and beyond. Then came a longer intermission, this time it stayed long enough to see who it was. 'God, isn't that the Home Secretary? Blurted out Carn as an image of a number of men all with mud on their knees standing amongst a flock of clearly disturbed sheep came up on screen. 'That's the Foreign Secretary too,' he continued.

'Perhaps that big bloke with the 9 mm pistol made them do it,' suggested the controller.

As their bulging disbelieving eyes became accustomed to the dark image of the barn it became apparent that the sick swine were performing to an audience, there being dozens of silent awe struck faces staring on from the straw bales at the back of the barn.

'No wonder the Government wanted to be kept out of the news,' thought Sir Hugh as he made for home, he didn't want to get involved in this mess, time to take a short holiday.

Damien couldn't wait to make his way home too but not until he'd started a law suit to protect his image. . . and perhaps make a few bob on the way.

**

For three days the news was filled with speculation and denials then lucky for the Government something else cropped up to take the attention. An Orang-utan had given birth to quadruplets in a laboratory experiment to solve the imminent extinction of the species. It was sponsored by the big Palm Oil conglomerate Grabitall Inc. Such wonderful news gave the Government a brief respite.

**

Addendum:

A few months later, the Government was overthrown in a landslide victory for anyone but them.

Sir Hugh 'Peregrine' Braggington Havalot was retired on a huge bonus and elevated to the Lords by the incoming coalition. His hopes of sleeping in ermine and dreaming of expenses came true.

Ms Bo, Boedica Flabergast was offered a multi million contract for the sole rights to her memoirs. As part of the conditions she was to write more books from a cottage on St Kilda Island. None of her work ever saw light of day, nor did she.

Rob 'mad marine' Oakes moved to the Merry Shepherd to woo the landlady and lived happy ever after.

Nigel Yorner was over his depression, why should he be depressed once he'd seen what a total mess everyone else was in, he went on to be a successful stand up comic doing the pubs and clubs of Landsovgrotty.

Skunk 'Spielberg' Harrison took up a fantastic offer to produce and direct an epic foreign film set in the east at an organic pig farm. He may be gone for some while.

Pretty blonde Samantha Wilfershore remained blissfully unaware of anything that was going on, anywhere, and was promoted to political editor of News Tripe the Corporation's flagship daily news magazine programme.

David 'Genghis' Carn was made redundant and once no longer associated with the Corporation was arrested, convicted and now serving four years in Dartmoor.

McTaggart the farmer started a tourism business and made a small fortune from guided tours and cafes all run by very economical employees with foreign accents and wearing sheep costumes. A speciality trip was to spend a night in the infamous barn itself. A small gift shop sold miniature stuffed sheep pub signs, and lots of sheep oriented cheap gifts.

Wallace the Rotweiller-Collie cross found himself enjoying spells of the well fed good life at a stud farm for the guard dog industry.

After the Government set up an inquiry into finding a panel to examine what should be the scope of any investigation, preferably taking so long that the guilty would have died of old age by then, the third inquiry decided it was too complex and should be considered for a public inquiry at the Home Secretary's discretion.

The disgraced Home Secretary and Foreign Secretary were both sentenced to ten years for various unmentionable crimes but simply served six months, just long enough to write a best selling novel each before being released. They now work as substantially paid consultants to the new Government. Who knows, if they do well, they may be wearing ermine one day too. You'll often see them on the telly.

How did you do out of it?

**

'If you keep hanging on to who you were,
you'll never become who you might be.'
**

26

Gibbet Hill
Psychiatric home for the gifted

A short play

THE CAST

Chairman. Doctor Lockemup. Self interested son of a vicious entrepreneur. Only in the job for the money.

The Nurse. Miss Lovemall. A kindly lady from a sheltered upbringing in a remote village with a loving family. Would gladly work for free.

The Psychiatrist. Reverend Snitcher, Dip H Licentiate of Psychology Institute of Cambodia. Had grown up with a brutal father where he was exposed to books on Freud, which his mother was using to try and understand her husband. He'd taken a keen interest in religion and psychology following his own first treatments.

The Client. A patient or a nutter, depending on your point of view. An old chap by name of Aidi Mwar.

A MEETING

Reason for meeting is a release application. First to give evidence is Nurse Lovemall.

Nurse Lovemall: 'Such a dear old gentleman; just taken up painting and produced this beautiful, blue coloured picture of someone walking free in life – climbing the steps into the light. He's a prime candidate for release.'

Doctor Lockemup: Makes a cursory note, before asking, 'What do you say Reverend Snitcher?'

Reverend Snitcher: 'An interesting insight into the subconscious of this morbid individual. Note that he is a loner. He's removed, possibly killed, all the other people that should be with him on these steps. Not only that, even on a sunny day, as he shows, his paranoia for self protection has made him paint an umbrella. It looks like he's carrying a handbag, too, of some description. And his knees are too close together. Note the big shadow – this is his inner psyche – dark and malevolent, reaching back into the darkness for which he longs. No. This is the painting of a deranged psychotic, perhaps, even psychopathic individual. The decision is yours though, Doctor. I'd say better safe than sorry.'

The Doctor twitches nervously under the intimidating stare of the Reverend.

Doctor Lockemup: 'Request for release denied. Next review scheduled in ten years. Meeting adjourned.'

(They all knew Aidi Mwar would be conveniently dead by then, that Nurse Lovemall would have retired to a puppy farm in the country and Doctor Lockemup would be in charge of some bigger institution, where he would be paid more and be on bonus for every inmate kept. The Reverend Snitcher would either be in prison – or politics.)

**

'Madness is rare in individuals – but in groups, parties, nations, and ages it is the rule.' Friedrich Nietzsche

**

27

A Football Match to end all Football Matches

The ever kindly residents of Wendymerton village were buzzing with childlike excitement. Their beautiful foundling football team, the 'Wendies' had made it big. They'd won promotion into the prestigious Bailiff's League, whose main sponsor was a ruthless debt collection agency.

They had never played with the 'big boys' before and were looking forward to showing off their skills on the same pitch as adorned by the much-admired footballing stars from other teams in the league. A dream come true.

Down in the village nerve centre, the Wendy Arms pub, one old timer asked, 'Do you think Beckam will be playing?'

'No, I think he's retired now but some of his old team mates play,' came a confident if slurred reply from another old timer. Neither had any idea about football outside of the village.

Their first game was going to be a treat, it was away and that meant a rare holiday for all. Some in the village had never yet left it to see the outside world.

Team and supporters would share the same coach, supplied by vintage enthusiast Monty Goodchap of the nearby village of Elpumawl. Even among those who had no interest in football there was keen competition for coach seats, mostly because it was heavily subsidised by tax-evading expenses from the Bailiff's League.

Finally the morning came for their eagerly awaited debut league match, an away game against another team of more seasoned hopefuls that hailed from Bressumer Slag, so named after the derelict steel works upon which their village was built.

They queued politely but excitedly to step aboard Goodchap's old but clean coach, its fine condition testament to a regular polish every Sunday morning before dinner. The team's manager mumbled a shy briefing to his 'lads'. He'd only held the post because he was retired and his cousin was the landlord. 'Enjoy the game lads; that's the most important thing,' he said, not realising that 'survive' might have been more pertinent advice. He further speculated, 'I hear that they have some foreign players, possibly top men from Europe or South America. You know, like Man City and the like have. Oh, and we must give a vote of thanks to the Women's Institute for supplying packed lunches for half time, it includes some of Miss Plumpley's traditional suet treacle pudding. Very nice too, I'm sure.'

It was a lovely sunny day as that happy and hopeful band set off through the rolling tree clad hills of their homeland.

Meanwhile, in the rain sodden grey of Bressumer Slag, the groundsman was herding some semi conscious sheep off the pitch. Behind him, a couple of extremely reluctant ball boys were cleaning up after them – and not very effectively either.

'They won't notice these little bits of dung amongst the divots and nettles,' said Lurcher the taller of the two.

'Nah, you're right Lurch, if they stay on their feet they'll be okay and anyway I hear they are country boys – they'll be well used to it, probably a deodorant for them,' replied Brutus, the shorter and better educated of the two – and the son of the goalkeeper, or so rumour had it. The images created in their 'unusual' minds had cheered them up and, leaving plenty of sheep dung behind them, they left the pitch to throw the dirty spades into an even dirtier shed.

Bressumer Slag's team manager was one sly and conniving old fox and had a trick or two up his sleeve to place the visitors at disadvantage. (Ever wondered why a home game is worth an extra goal or more?) His name was 'John Smith', not his real name of course but in his line of business he'd found it prudent if not essential to remain incognito. John checked with his grounds-man, a local down and out who only answered to Billy and who lived rent free in the shed at the ground in return for his labours. Remember the sheep? They weren't his. . . he'd sort of just 'borrowed' them.

'Now, my son, (and who knows, he might have been) don't forget to make sure the toilets at the away end aren't clean. Put this sign up on the door.' John could see Billy struggling with the words, 'Don't worry what it says; just nail it to the door. . . this way up!' he said, turning the sign around in Billy's hands.

AWAY TEAM CHANGING ROOM

Due to several previous thefts the management of
Bressumer Slag Football Team cannot accept any liability.
You are advised to carry your belongings with you.
This door must not be locked as this is also a Public Toilet

'And Billy, you make sure their coach has to park at the far end of the ground, near that boggy bit. Don't help them to find their way into the ground either,' John said, slipping Billy enough money to buy a couple of cheap Lagers.

Billy nodded and smiled. Visiting clubs had always been a good little earner for him in the past, in more ways than most people would ever guess.

The away end at Bressumer Slag was so called because any one with any sense, including sense of smell, kept away from it, mainly due to the noxious fumes that emanated from the earth from time to time. Let's face it, the only reason the team occupied the ground was because no planning permission could ever be granted over the old steel works former waste pit. (The sheep didn't look too healthy on it either but it didn't bother Billy over much as they were mostly destined for the away-end meat pies.)

The away-end stand was constructed mainly of corroded corrugated iron sheeting, even the once galvanised metal hand rails were corroded. No grass or moss grew within several yards of the dilapidated structure. In fact most of the goal mouth grass also had a deathly yellow tinge and the posts and nets had to be replaced every year.

The visiting supporter's food came from a burger van made from a converted caravan that had once been abandoned by some unfortunate holiday makers that had strayed by accident into Bressumer Slag. (At their bedside in rehab they had signed a possession waiver to Bressumer Slag's representative. John Smith accommodatingly told them to leave the name blank and he would fill it in later, he was good like that!) The burger van was 'manned' by a little old deaf lady known affectionately to the locals as Lucrezia. She suffered with virulent dermatitis and frequently sneezed or coughed into her well worn and unwashed apron.

Goodchap's coach duly pulled in to the car park and was marshalled painfully and rather slowly to the boggy end. The coach arrived with a row of horrified faces staring in disbelief from the windows, faces that looked more like they were arriving at a concentration camp than a football stadium. As the occupants disembarked into a great puddle, organised courtesy of Billy the groundsman, some tried to stay on board. . . including a couple of their least valiant players! I mean, they were in the team to enjoy the beer and footy not to visit some death camp.

Eventually, after having been sent the wrong way several times, they settled into their changing room - the windowless away end toilet block. Settled perhaps is the wrong word because changing clothes on a urine soaked floor presented its own set of difficulties for their once clean socked feet. More than one ended up hopping about on one boot and sending panic stricken team mates into their own and often highly inelegant and unsuccessful hopping frenzy. Once changed and liberally reeking of stale urine, mostly Billy's, they carried their bags outside, accompanied by several resident flies. On reaching the grey and strange smelling air, a couple of the flies dropped dead from fume inhalation. The team reluctantly and cautiously piled up their urine sodden bags in a heap. . . closely watched by an astutely vigilant Billy, who had long taken a keen interest in security. . . other people's mostly.

The visiting team's dug out was exactly what it said it was, a hole dug out and furnished with one of those cheap, white when new but later mildewed patio chairs and a bailing bucket, which had many times found other uses. In front of his dugout Marcus Blagalot-Smythe the Wendies' manager couldn't help notice the mound of soil which obscured his view of parts of the pitch, it didn't escape his attention either how much it looked like a fresh grave. . . all it needed was an inscribed tomb-stone at one end to complete the picture.

From the dubious comfort of the derelict away end, visiting supporters could feast their frequently watering eyes on the plush modernised 'home end' with its fine seating, clean toilets, several bars and a state of the art food kiosk, which even boasted a nicely framed hygiene certificate.

Eventually, when the game was all set to start, Bressumer Slag's striker, a thug of a man about eighteen stone and known only as 'Basher', was missing. The referee soon spotted him on the touch line trying to sell drugs to the stewards. Blowing his whistle hard three times then stopping for a brief cough, he shouted above the baying home crowd's insulting chants, 'Oi, Basher, get yourself on the pitch we're waiting on you.'

'Keep yer 'air on cousin, I'm coming,' retorted a sneering Basher, a local entrepreneur of sorts and whose wife was down at the away end selling air fresheners and sick bags. . . always a good seller and a roaring trade on a good day. Apart from the odd visiting convict and illegal immigrant most of the team were related in some way, by blood, marriage or suspicion.

The Bressumer Slag team hardly ever went down the away-end. When forced by rules, they despised and mostly ignored, to play from that half of the pitch the entire team including the goal keeper migrated to the home end, where they scored all their goals. It was on record that never had they scored a goal in the away end. . . oh, there was one time, an own goal it was, the visiting goalkeeper had collapsed with food poisoning or possibly gassing and in dropping the ball it had rolled into the net. 'They all count', was their motto, and they didn't much care how they got them either, as the naive Wendies were about to find out much to their cost.

Somehow, and known only to the referee and the skipper of Bressumer Slag, they always won the toss and chose to start from the home end which they defended tooth and nail. . . often quite literally. This kept the opposition hemmed in to the away end and the hallucinating and debilitating effects of mind and lung changing fumes that pervaded that end of the pitch. So bad was the effect that the opposition never noticed the sheep dung or the nettles, well, not until later and usually only on the coach or after they came around at home. It also meant that by half time there was little life or ambition in any opposing team, leaving them easy prey for the rampant 'Hyenas', Bressumer Slag's nickname; chosen by popular local vote. Other names rejected in the vote were, 'Slags', 'Grey Devils', named after their all grey football strip. . . selected for the characteristics of infrequent washing, 'Vultures', came a close second in the poll and 'Scrappies', after the dubious scrap metal deals that had forged some of the village fortunes.

The Wendies, despite desperate cheering from their steadily weakening and now frail supporters, failed to penetrate the stoutly defensive wall of sub human flesh and bone epitomized by the Bressumer Slag forward and midfield players.

(The author takes a moment to consider the choice of the word 'players'. It carries the connotation of a game; a game often played with gusto but tinged with sportsmanship. The Bressumer Slag team was made up of Mafiosa wannabees, psychopaths that had so far avoided detection and treatment, opportunists, muggers, one or two playing only to have their passports returned and inmates from the local open prison. When you, the reader, encounter the word player in relation to a 'Hyenas" team member, please don't be taken in.)

Years of intimidation, robbery, poaching, debt collecting and occasional prison brawls had honed the forwards and midfield into a formidable fighting force – definitely not what the sporting amateurs of Wendymerton were expecting at all.

The Wendies' forward players, including Niles and Quentin, were less affected by the away end fumes and their associated anaesthetic qualities and in consequence felt every crunching tackle meted out. Tackles went in, ball or not; however, the Wendies were quite pleased with their proportion of possession, it was almost as though the 'Hyenas' wanted them to have the ball. And they did too – anyone with the ball was fair game. It was in the Hyenas' blood; any local game was chased, snared or shot. In fact their manager had briefly considered some of these options on the pitch but was dissuaded by his psychiatrist and Big Sid, his brother-in-law and local magistrate.

Legs and arms covered in bruises and tiny white bumps from falling into the short, genetically adapted stinging nettle beds of the Hyenas' pitch and smelling of stuff that they hadn't yet identified except it abused their nostrils, the forwards began to lose hope. Some of them were to lose more than that by the end of the day. Some of them lost consciousness from clandestine elbows on the referee's blind side, after which the Hyenas' player would scream and fall to the floor clutching his groin and writhing in brilliantly simulated pain. The result was always a yellow card to the unconscious Wendy. Twice in the second half the referee used his foot to roll the body over to obtain the player's number.

Of course, first aid was available as it was league rules. First Aid was supplied by the home team and was made up of two very keen volunteers. One was a chap with a reputed IQ of nearly 30 and who had subsequently been denied the medical school place to which he believed he was entitled – he wanted to be a Doctor. Being a volunteer First Aider was the next best thing, as it gave his totally untrained hands and mind an unfettered and steady supply of victims for experiment. The 'Doctor's' colleague, known only for some spurious reason as Gerbils, was a strange chap who had frequently and voluntarily been the pleasured recipient of medical treatment in Nuttington Mental Institute over many years. The less said about him the better as it might further traumatise any of the Wendymerton players unlucky enough to have been 'treated' by him; apparently, Broderick, Wendies' left back is still receiving therapy for his disturbing nightmares. The First Aid team were equipped with a variety of instruments, equipment and certificates, all curiously, but never questioned, marked with 'Property of Nuttington M. Inst.'

The referee did little to intervene, I mean, it wasn't his place to do so, was it? Medical attention wasn't his remit, managing the football team – I mean football match - *was*.

His linesmen weren't all there either. . . in more ways than one. Once, on looking up for help with a touch line decision the referee noticed his linesman was missing – well, not so much missing but to be found at the home end food bar collecting his salmon and coriander butter panini. The decision went against the Wendies of course. They didn't complain as all their previous pleas for justice were met with warnings or yellow cards. They needed every player they had - just to stay alive, never mind win a game.

The local press never attended, they were in fact actively dissuaded from doing so. Bressumer Slag always issued a post match press release for publication. The local readers were always pleased with the reports on their team's progress in the league; an example follows:-

'Despite facing a blatantly evil and frequently cheating
opposition, many of them on steroids or worse,
fortune favoured the brave players of Bressumer Slag,
who with fair play and sportsmanship to the fore used
sporting prowess and skill to snatch a glorious victory.
Bressumer Slag, 8, Little Wimpington, 0'

There were never any photographs of the game, half the team were 'camera shy' (read: 'wanted') and others were quote, 'Not seeking praise or publicity for their good work on behalf of the village.'

As regards the local press, Bressumer Slag had a 'gentleman's agreement' with the local editor. He didn't write anything bad about them and they in turn would not dognap his pet, dress it up in a dead badger skin and use it for sport. The editor was well aware of the power wielded by the local football team as his paper had featured many of the players' court appearances.

Everything went to plan for the Hyenas and nobody could take that from them. They were indeed a team, a powerful team forged in life to take on all-comers and to use everything in their collective arsenal to destroy the enemy; today it was the Wendies! Management ruled like hardened dictators and made an example of the team and its functionaries with draconian brutality.

Meanwhile back in the game, something very rarely seen was to bring the crowd to its feet. There was a faint glimmer of hope when the Wendies' star striker, Jasper Giles, jinked his way like a rabbit on fire past the brutal midfielders and closed to within shooting range only moments before the left back's right boot acquainted itself with his testicles. . . at some considerable velocity. The blood-curdling scream would have enhanced any Spielburg horror movie. The referee reluctantly ordered a free kick to the Wendies and had a very strong 'reprimanding' word with the offender, 'Sorry about the free kick mate, don't make it so obvious next time. . . that's if there's anyone left standing to play.'

To consider their best options, a collective of Wendies' senior players, Broderick, Dorian and Horatio gathered by the dead ball, (words not lost on their star striker who was now currently and quite publicly engrossed in examining his testicles with great care and attention. In any case he was in no fit state to take any free kick). A set piece was their best chance, mainly as it didn't involve having to run anywhere, a skill they'd lost within twenty minutes of the first whistle. Wendies' striking force, if it could be called that, decided to put their biggest player near the goal mouth and hope for a header on target. Archie was the tallest by far, well over six feet but only weighing in at eleven stone. 'Archie, you know what to do, we'll fool the dopes with a couple of passes here and with a dummy run from Tarquin we can lob the ball your way, it's up to you. . . the honour of our club and our village is at stake. No pressure. Watch out for the left back, the guy with the tattoos and scars, he doesn't look all there.' They all slapped Archie on the back with a smile and in so doing gave away their plan, not that it would make any difference as Archie ended up being punishingly crushed at speed, an accident naturally, between the sixteen stone Goalkeeper, Jock of Barlinney and the sixteen stone right back Bones McGraw on loan from an ex-Parkhust eleven. The semi-conscious Archie was stretchered off to the rapturous applause of the home supporters who were enjoying a well played seven nil game and all the fringe entertainments. Some supporters didn't mind the goals scored it was a good ratio of stretcher cases they'd come to see. A happy bunch they were today for sure and definitely had their money's worth against the Wendies.

The Wendies were down to nine men on the field, seven of them with dubious yellow cards to their names. From his dugout, a resemblance to a 1914-1918 front line trench now being a bonus not a defect, the Wendys' manager, while hurriedly formulating his imminent resignation speech scanned his limited view of the Bressumer Slag horizon for his substitutes but none could be found. Suspicion never fell on Billy, as player discretion (read cowardice) seemed a more plausible cause.

Bressumer Slags' midfield defender, a euphemism if ever there was one, by name of Ivor Hatchet, *(tell me, that can't be his real name, surely)* needed to leave the pitch as his curfew was due . . . most of the opposition he made contact with had sensed their own version of a curfew. As all Bressumer Slags' substitutes were by now the worse for celebratory drinks the referee had to find an excuse to send him off. Ivor was only on day release from the local prison and couldn't afford to upset the authorities because as their most efficient and ruthless midfielder he was needed for the next games. There was a limit to Bressumer Slag's power after all.

***

After the game was over and well and truly lost, the tattered remnants of a once happy village team gathered at the coach, which was in the process of being towed out of the soft ground by a digger that belonged to the referee's brother. Monty thought that £50 was cheap enough for the villagers' freedom and his coach back and he thought that the graffiti might well come off with some cutting polish. As the villagers took their seats on board amid the stench of old urine, sheep dung and toxic steel works' waste, Monty Goodchap set off for the local hospital to pick up three of their players from A&E. As he left the car park he was shocked by how little diesel he had left in the tank, he was sure it had been more than half full when they arrived. To be on the safe side he fuelled up at Bressumer Slag's only and extortionately expensive garage, incidentally owned by a hefty brute of a woman with a skull and crossbones tattoo; it was John Smith's dear old mother, Brutina Smith.

It was a match to end all matches. It certainly ended any dreams for Wendymerton.

Ah, the beautiful game.

**

*'Do not seek to follow in the footsteps of the wise,
seek what they sought.'*

**

*'And there was joy in the home of the Ravens that their young
would eat their fill.'*

28

The Dining Out Night

For the young couple in their early twenties it was their first
date and they had chosen a pleasant little restaurant in a trouble
-free part of town and which had tasteful lighting and secretive,
discreetly placed tables. The Manager ushered them to a fine
table, complete with candles and real flowers in a pretty vase,
'There you are sir and madam, your waiter will be with you
shortly, do have a lovely evening.'

The menu was examined, choices made and the food duly
brought by the waiter. The young man's hobbies, beliefs and
allegiances to various, seemingly extreme groups intrigued the
young lady and, as they began their main course, she sought
his opinion on a certain matter that had concerned her in the
past. . .

He thought carefully for what seemed like an age, before answering, 'Well, as you asked, and obviously want to hear the
truth,' he said, 'it probably went something like this. . . I'd say
she was probably not very old but in her few years of God-given
freedom had seen wonders that we can't even dream of on this
Earth; she knew secrets we can never share. Then fate, thinly
disguised as man, cruelly and abruptly wrenched her from the
only home she knew or ever could know. She almost certainly
put up a desperate struggle and feared for her life. It would
have been hopeless, she would have been powerless to save herself, and she would have gasped for a breath that was never to
be hers again. All around her would lay the dead and still

dying. . . many of them her own kin. No one would hear her cries for help and few really would have cared.'

She threw down her knife and fork and with tears in her eyes, and standing, looked angrily into his face, 'How could you? I can't eat this now!'

'Excuse me madam but is there something wrong with the fish?' the waiter inquired.

**

'A wise man hears one word but understands two.'
**

29

Christmas Dinner - The Invitation

It seemed impolite, not to accept the old couple's invitation to join them for Christmas dinner. Many years of living alone had made him resigned to doing his usual thing but for a change he thought he'd take up their kindly offer, despite only having met them at the bus stop the day before.

He arrived as requested, just before mid-day. The old man, Bert, opened the door to him and with a squint into the brightness of normal daylight, grudgingly accepted the chocolates and wine and stood to one side. He was met by a mixture of strange odours, the overriding one emanating from the kitchen was a distinct burnt smell.

'Come on through,' said Bert, 'keep the warmth in. We don't open our windows till May - last year it wasn't till June. No, keep yer shoes on. . . or her damn dog'll 'ave 'em else.'

As his eyes slowly became accustomed to the semi-gloom he was glad he'd kept his shoes on: the living room floor was littered with things the dog had encountered in the months and even years gone by. Bert used a stained, slippered foot to slide a full cat litter tray under a coffee table. 'Sit yerself down and make yerself comfortable. I'll go and tell herself you've arrived.'

He carefully chose the only chair that wasn't cluttered and sat down. He noted the décor, the like of which he'd not seen since his great uncle had passed away. As he heard a toilet flush somewhere in the house, a large long haired and unkempt brown dog rushed into the room and shoved its wet nose straight into his groin. As he struggled to push the excited animal away, 'herself' came into the room holding out a wet hand to shake his.

'Bert,' she scolded, 'you should have told him not to sit there.' As he stood from the chair, his backside felt a little damp. Herself continued, 'His damn cat wet itself there yesterday.' She brushed her hand over the now warm dampness, 'Not to worry, nearly dry now. Come on through and sit at the table.'

'Bert! For God's sake, don't let the dog do that! It's disgusting at dinner time.'

He was beginning to regret coming, life was better at home, still, perhaps the dinner would be good, I mean they couldn't have reached that age on bad food. 'You're worrying over nothing,' he told himself as he squeezed by the dog that had now transferred it's attention to twenty quid's worth of M&S chocolates which it eagerly bolted down, complete with wrappers.

What a relief, he needn't have worried, the table was set with bright clean cutlery and crockery. 'I bet they have a dish washer out back,' he thought, thinking further that it was an appliance he had long admired though never bought.

'You sit yourself at the head of the table dear. . . Bert! Throw that damn cat out into the garden.' Herself's tone softened and continued, 'I've already had to change the menu once today, the blessed thing mauled and gummed about the chicken breast I'd taken out of the freezer. Try as I might, just couldn't save it I'm afraid. . . we've got sausages now. I take it you like sausages?'

Well this was going to be one novel Christmas dinner; one he'd never dreamed of and, nor likely, would anyone else. 'Yes, sausages will be fine, are they beef or pork?' he enquired, in as matter of fact tone as he could muster.

'Neither I think,' herself replied, brushing something indescribable off of her apron. 'We got a job-lot off a traveller last year, he said they were venison. Could be or could be rabbit or perhaps even cat . . .' she laughed. 'Pity they didn't take Bert's old Fluffy at the same time.'

Candles lit in the table centre added a festive feel to the place, as well as a little warmth and were a welcome insurance against darkness should the electric meter run out.

It was quite a posh set up with the food in large bowls from which you served yourself. 'Don't be shy, get stuck in,' she said, slapping Bert's hand, 'let the gentleman go first, you wait your turn.'

Carefully, trying to take from the middles, he selected small portions of what transpired to be margarine and turnip mash, last year's de-frozen Brussels sprouts, a dark green cabbage with the most un-chewable leaves he'd ever encountered and some small roasted potatoes, which actually seemed the best bet there, so he took extras. Bert smiled with pride as he watched his guest load up on roast potatoes, he'd dug them himself. Free they were, growing wild down by the sewage outfall. Must have been dumped at some time then self-propagated from then on. Easy to dig too.

Herself lifted the lid on an old enamelled casserole dish to expose several burnt sausages. 'They're nice and well cooked, you can never be too careful with sausages I say.' She put three on his plate, three for Bert and two for herself, saving one for the dog. 'I told Bert to put them in the fridge but thick that he is, he left them out in a warm kitchen overnight. . . I knew I should have done it myself.' She concluded her verbal assassination with a sigh.

As he ate those bits he'd chosen for his plate and that looked almost edible and hacked the burnt crust off the curious tasting sausages, he felt his right foot becoming wet. His first thought was the cat had somehow sneaked back in but looking down, saw that it was the half retching dog, an excess of anticipatory drool flowing steadily from open, chocolate covered jaws onto his socks and best suede shoes.

As he thought deeply about the foolishness of accepting this invite, he was shaken out of his mindful solitude by herself saying loudly, 'Eat up, there's plenty more, and I've made my own Christmas pudding, Bert even found some loose change in his pocket to put in there, so if you are lucky you could be going home with more than you came with.'

He felt his tummy rumble and watched as a large flea performed a double somersault on the way from dog to damp sock. 'Yes,' he thought, 'I'm sure you are right there.'

He looked at his watch and with pretence shock, yelled, 'Oh dear, I'm so sorry, is that the time, I just remembered I have to be home for a very important phone call. I'm sorry to dash off - it was really nice, thank you.'

'Would you like me to make up a doggy bag for your tea?' Herself asked kindly.

When he graciously declined, she scraped the remaining bits of sausage onto Bert's plate and then placed it on the floor in front of an apparently ravenous brown dog, which in turn was probably feeding a couple of well established tape worms. As he stood in the doorway he watched in stunned silence as herself picked up the now spotlessly clean plate from the floor and placed it back on the table. 'There,' she said, 'clean as a whistle and did you know, a dog's saliva is antibacterial. Almost better than a dishwasher Bert says. . . and a lot cheaper.'

As he waved his goodbyes to an already closing door he wondered if the doctor's surgery might be running an emergency service, now all he had to do was make it back home and find out.

Happy Christmas, and by the way, what are you doing for dinner?

30

An Old Enemy and the Valentine's Day Taxi.
A short story constructed using the words in the title for a writing group exercise.

He was a romantic deep at heart, enamoured with plans and day-dreams of how life should play out. Unfortunately two things usually went wrong - making the plan fit the dream and finding someone that actually fitted the plan. Eventually he turned to the internet, discovering many exciting people; but one in particular had invariably responded positively with his every suggestion. This was his dream come true and he couldn't wait to meet her, for she had charmed him with her sweet answers. Of course, you can't be too careful on the internet and he was wary enough to cloak his true feelings in a web of innuendo and blatant story telling. However, he felt total trust in her revealing and beautiful replies.

Today was the day – Valentine's Day - 'No, damn Valentine,' he thought, 'this is my day.' Having met someone special on line he was besotted with the image he had created in his mind of the new 'Lorna Doone' in his life. He'd bought some new clothes, possibly never to be worn again but bought especially for this, the night his dreams would come true.

The restaurant was booked. He'd already paid a non refundable £50 deposit, 'What's money,' he thought, 'compared to living your dreams.'

At six pm he'd been dressed ready for at least a couple of hours and paced the living room of his little terraced house, fondling a small gold locket in his pocket. A gift, a small trinket, for the besotted one's new love in life. Gold it was, but what's money compared to dreams eh?

At about six thirty he wondered if the taxi would ever arrive. He worried a lot. He drifted into one of his perfect dreams, perfection, none better. . . his hands reaching across the table, gently caressed by the radiant, adorable and ever loving 'Lorna Doone' – a gentle soul full of love and kindness, talented and strong but ever willing to listen to and be guided by his wisdoms, for he would be all the world to her. . .   ahh, such dreams. At seven pm the taxi arrived. . . on time.

He sat in the front seat, 'Maxime's Restaurant please,' he proclaimed with pride, for he'd never done much better than a chip shop before.

'Certainly sir,' replied the over- courteous driver as he eagerly pressed the start button of his money making meter and drove rather slowly away from the house and in the wrong direction – he knew a scenic route to Maxime's.

'We avoid the road works this way sir and there's been an accident in town; a pork scratchings lorry's lost its load swerving to avoid a drunk on a stolen bike. Lovely route this, all my fares say how much they like it.'

Thirty minutes later into the five minute trip and thirty seven pounds and fifty three pence to the poorer, they arrived and he made his way to reception.

Being greeted politely by the suitably elegant and efficient manager, he gave his name and his booking for two. 'Ah, yes sir, your 'friend' arrived earlier, I've taken the liberty of putting you in one of the private booths, out of sight. . . I mean, give you some privacy. . . I'm sure that is what you would want, sir,' said the manager in discreet but knowing tones.

He was ushered to a booth and as the blue velvet curtain was drawn back he intentionally did not look up. As he stepped in and took his seat he kept his eyes down, his dreams were filling him with the wildest of anticipations, he prepared for the mesmerising vision of beauty he was about to behold.

A gruff middle aged voice wearing bib and brace overalls and sporting a lager soaked beard shook him to the core, 'hello mate, you must be Mervin, I'm Nigel, a scaffolder from Sheffield, just love all your twisted little innuendos. . . couldn't wait to meet you. . . aren't you the clever one. . .'

He wasn't listening. Making his excuses, if any were ever needed, he almost pulled the curtain off its rails in his hurry to leave.

As he passed by reception the manager calmly enquired with a measured amount of stoicism, 'Leaving so early sir? Was everything alright? Hope to see you again sir.'

He didn't hear any of it, he just hoped upon hope that the guy from 'Ageing Tortoise' taxis was still outside. Of course he wasn't. Taxis only drive slowly when they have a fare, otherwise, the term 'bats from hell' is more appropriate.

Never mind, with armpits now soaked in the sweat of fear, he found another just around the corner. '72 Blogg Street and can you hurry please.'

'Can't go straight there sir,' explained the ever helpful taxi driver, 'Been an incident in town; animal rights nutters released everything from that big pet supermarket, town's overrun with gerbils, ferrets, scorpions and the like, police with tranquilliser guns been in action. . . . shot the shop owner. I'll take you the scenic route, most of my fares say they like it.'

Some new clothes, fifty quid and twice thirty seven pounds and fifty three pence to the poorer, he entered his little house, drew the curtains firmly against prying eyes and put on the light. As he looked across the room his old enemy stood there, unsmiling, giving him a vacant forlorn stare.

'You dopey burke,' he said to the mirror.

**

'If you don't keep quiet, you will never hear the echo.'

**

31

Mrs Hoblingsgote – medical expert.

'Your favourite patient to see you doctor,' sighed the exasperated medical receptionist as she reported the third visit that week to Dr Hadenuff by Mrs Hipaemia Hoblingsgote.

'Send her through then, Miss Tattle. Let us see what she's "caught" this time.' The doctor, threw an extra tranquiliser down his throat followed quickly by some experimental super juice on trial for mental disorders.

Mrs Hoblingsgote was the local hypochondriac; her Christian name had been adulterated by her very small circle of friends to 'Hypo' and she was well known throughout the county medical services. She'd been tested for anything from Dengue fever, rabies, osteo degeneration of brain tissue, green monkey disease and several other tropical diseases she'd read about in the papers or any one of the several medical journals to which she subscribed. Until the editors worked out that her qualifications were merely a figment of their own imaginations, they used to publish her letters and articles. Despite never having left the county except for a visit to London to see a hypnotherapy specialist she was convinced that most sufferers of illness were being let down by the wilful misdiagnosis of medical practitioners under government orders to suppress the real truth. After her visit the hypnotherapist retired on ill health and now runs a gerbil farm on an isolated Greek island.

'What is it today then Mrs Hoblingsgote? Bubonic plague?' the Doctor inwardly sneered with sarcasm while forcing his face to contort into the bedside smile he'd been taught at medical school, a valued skill that attracted the highest of marks in the practical exam, as he recalled.

'Ah, Doctor Hadenuff,' replied Mrs Hoblingsgote, in a dubious tone that questioned not only the doctor's sincerity but his qualification in anything medical. 'I'm feeling a pulse in the centre of my forehead and an examination of blood vessels and circulation, conducted through Google (read 'God' in her eyes) indicates this should not be possible. Either one of my veins has slipped or some flesh eating creature with a pulse has burrowed into my skin.' Dr Hadenuff sighed inwardly, he knew best not to argue directly as he'd been the subject of several reports to the medical council already. He picked up his stethoscope and walked around behind his patient, wondering how many years he'd get if he strangled her with it. Fortunately the cognitive behavioural therapy on which he had been placed by desperate employers not wishing to inflict Mrs Hoblingsgote on any one else in the practice, kicked in and he placed the listening end of the equipment on her forehead.

She turned sharply pulling it from his hand and shouting down it that it was cold and any doctor worth his salt would have warmed it first. By now the doctor wouldn't have heard a pulse even if there was one but he knew he must not give up. Until she was satisfied with an answer she would not leave his surgery. 'No pulse that I can find Mrs Hoblingsgote, show me how you found it yourself,' he said with pseudo pleasantness, a ploy that seemed to have worked in the past.

'Like this Doctor (read 'Dopey'),' she shouted as though he was deaf and thrusting her thumb into the middle of her forehead, her face silently asking the question, 'well, what have you got to say now then thicky?'

'Ah, Mrs Hoblingsgote, a common mistake,' adding very quickly so she couldn't take offence, 'even by members of skilled medical staff at times I'm told, there is a pulse in the thumb itself and that is what you feel when you press it against your forehead (read, 'your thick skull you time wasting nit wit').

Mrs Hoblingsgote wasn't convinced, Google had never been wrong before, but she had to leave for an appointment with a

Tarot reader before going on to the 'Pensioners against euthanasia' group of which she was a most active and vociferous chair. She'd probably report the doctor's incompetence later, unless of course the rampant dementia which she thought she'd had since childhood intervened. She thought she'd contracted it from a donkey bite when she was about twelve. The owner of the donkey sanctuary had reported the child's attack on his donkey to the RSPCA but no charges were pressed.

After the meeting Mrs Hoblingsgote donned her rucksack and jogged the two miles to the supermarket. While in there looking for bargains at the in store pharmacy, she ate three of the five pork pies she had purchased (well almost purchased anyway) a half of one of the cream cakes from the bakery, 'Mmm, chocolate éclairs. . . real cream. . . mmm', she mumbled to herself through a mouthful of cake and drool, and had a swig of expensive pomegranate juice. (She considered putting it back on the shelf but noticed she was being watched by well built security guard, 'fat git', she thought, ' could do with going on a diet.'

She paid for her shopping; loaded what was left of it into the rucksack and jogged back home. As she walked up the driveway past her newly polished car she looked at the disabled badge on the dash, thinking that it must be due for automatic renewal this month and it wouldn't be so long before her essential mobility car was up for replacement. She had thought about a Jaguar next but humility got the better of her and she set her heart on a BMW instead.

Shoving the last half of an éclair into her mouth she settled into her comfortable NHS orthopaedic chair and communed with God, that is she hit the Google connect button, there were things afoot she must investigate. . . like that hopeless quack telling her there was a pulse in the thumb for a start.

Mrs Hoblingsgote's computer held more medical information than the Lancet's archives and it was always willing to offer her more diseases to relish. She began to type in 'pu. . .' when it quickly offered her the opportunity to read about pulmonary oedema. She did not hesitate and within minutes of reading the preface she was choking and coughing like she'd been

gassed in the trenches. This was a hospital job for sure. . .
'Emergency, which service?' came the telephonist's reply.

Mrs Hoblingsgote gasped out with what seemed like a dying breath, 'Ambulance. . . gasp, wheeze, cough. . . another longer gasp.'

The novice telephonist put her through immediately to ambulance despatch. As the 'red' phone rang in ambulance control the electronic indicator informed the controller of the phone number being used. . . that too rang a bell. . . it was a number all too familiar to the ambulance service.

'Hello, you're through to ambulance control, name and telephone number please and what is the problem?' said old Chris, a veteran of the service for some thirty years.

Mrs Hoblingsgote was still taking in more information on her health problem from a link on the original article. She wheezed, coughed then went silent for a while before gasping out, 'urgent, pulmonary oedema, need urgent hospital treatment, need consultant in. . .'

Under strict orders to comply with turn-out times and thus satisfy attendance criteria for the government's big pre-election crackdown, Chris swung into action. 'Still at the old address Mrs Hoblingsgote?' A gasped 'yes' was all he needed to despatch the nearest ambulance to Nightingale Lodge, Bishop's Road. It didn't matter what sort of ambulance or who was on board, any old thing would do for the Nightingale Hypo as she was endearingly known, as long as it turned up and dropped her off at A&E and scored points for timeliness that is all that mattered. 'Ambulance on its way Mrs Hoblingsgote, just do the usual, be by the door with an overnight bag, tooth brush, nightie and the like, some coins for the hospital TV and a newspaper in the morning.'

As usual, Mrs Hoblingsgote was ready with her 'hospital gear' and even if she couldn't get to the door, all the emergency services knew where the door key was kept under the flowerpot to the left. It wasn't long, ensconced as she was in her usual ward bed, before she was coughing herself into a frenzy in front of the consultant and disturbing a ward full of genuinely ailing souls. The Hospital staff might have found her a burden but management almost looked forward to her visits as the turn around was quick and it made their admittance to discharge statistics look remarkably good. Good statistics meant a proportionate bigger bonus, not that that is why they did the job of course.

Next day, assured by a nervous gathering of as many doctors as they could find, by several X- rays and a promise of the first scan when the new equipment was purchased and a large bag of various drugs, Mrs Hoblingsgote strolled jauntily out to the waiting ambulance.

'Pity we can't euthanize her,' mumbled one doctor clenching his knuckles and who'd not had a minute to deal with anyone else all night.

'Any chance of popping in the newsagents for my paper?' she enquired, 'I don't think I'll be able to get about much today.'

The ambulance crew obliged. You never knew when the clients would be sent a customer survey as to how they were treated, and Mrs Hoblingsgote was someone to be reckoned with. . . she'd already had two nurses, a doctor and a car park attendant struck off.

After a big fried breakfast and her yoga session she settled down in her chair to watch some medical videos she'd picked up cheap in a charity shop. They looked promising as they included footage of real operations and bore an 18+ rating.

The door bell rang to the tune of 'The Sorcerer's Apprentice' causing Mrs Hoblingsgote to leap to her feet then limp gracefully and with all the aplomb of an Oscar winning actress to the front door. She opened it carefully and showed a face wizened with pain to the caller.

'Morning Mrs Hoblingsgote, it's only me, Phillipa, the assistant at the village pharmacy. Can you spare me a minute?'

'Come on in dear, you'll have to excuse the mess, just can't do it these days what with my troubles and all,' she said with a mild croak and an exaggerated limp. 'What can I do for you?'

Phillipa put on her best smile and said, 'Mr Scribblings the pharmacist is in need of your help. The pharmacy has run out of two drugs, tri-pheno-di-benzoquack and baboonazipan, Mr Scriblings wondered if you have any spare that you could lend us until next week when a delivery is expected from Hong Kong.'

Mrs Hoblingsgote groaned and made a fuss about standing from her chair, 'this way dear,' and she led Phillipa through to her own kitchen come dispensary. Opening one of the big cupboards to an amazing selection of life saving drugs, some still experimental and some still unopened in original packaging, 'help yourself dear, but mind you replace them next week, you never know when they might be needed.'

Phillipa selected the required drugs and placed them in a cool bag she had brought with her. Meanwhile, Mrs Hoblingsgote was reminiscing about previous pharmacists and counter staff, 'I knew your mother, dear, when she was at the pharmacy. Lovely lady, sorry to hear about her passing away, you look so much like her. . . lovely lady.'

Mrs Hoblingsgote had outlived several assistants, two pharmacists and the village postmaster. For such a frail and ill lady Mrs Hoblingsgote was managing extremely well, in fact, on her way to make medical history for surviving TB, scarlet fever, diphtheria, Ebola, black death and the virulent super bird flu mutation as well as numerous unknown diseases still being investigated.

'Bye bye Phillipa, nice to see you, must take my pills now and have a lie down before meals on wheels turn up,' she said with a limp wave goodbye from her front door.

'What a dear brave old lady,' thought Phillipa as she fought off the pain of her own debilitating arthritis while walking back to the pharmacy.

Mrs Hoblingsgote jogged jauntily upstairs to pack her suitcase, she'd been given a grant from a local charity to take a week's respite care at a private clinic in the Cotswolds but she'd managed to secretly exchange it for a bush craft week on the moors. (When man-made drugs had been used up or were too expensive to give away then she may have to turn to nature's healing ways and herbalism. This was a need to know mission).

Mrs Hoblingsgote was leading a double life if not a charmed one, though charm would not have been in the vocabulary of the myriad of health workers whose lives she had blighted and many of whom she had outlived, her cost to the NHS probably ran into millions especially when you took into account the ill health pensions and compensations paid out to those who crossed her hypocondriacal path. However, to the University of Kurdlingstahn she was a god send. As a senior consultant to the medical facility she had been given an honorary doctorate and was the main link between the university department of medicine and the west. She had designed and authorised many experiments on volunteers (read ethnic minorities and prisoners) in the development of her own theories on treating the anxious and depressed. She had several medical articles in her name but only in the Kurdlinstahny language, so ensuring anonymity.

A large bronze statue consisting of a recumbent goat and an elderly woman holding a stethoscope in one hand and a raised walking stick in the other, still adorns the main square of the capital city, Drugonia.

She is probably still alive and living in a town near you, you might know her, you might *be* her!

Rather light a candle than complain about the darkness.

32

Three Little Pigs.
(An alternative version of
a popular children's tale.)

Beautiful was that land, so full of life, so full of natural wonders. It was a paradise land, steeped in the millennia of natural history and yet still holding a golden promise far into a bright future.

Great forest trees flourished in their thousands, nurtured timelessly by Sun, air, earth and rain. The patchwork landscape of mountains and valleys blended in perfect harmony, lovingly sewn together by the silver threads of sparkling streams and rivers.

It was the land of nature itself and she lived there in peace with the animals and birds of the wilderness. It was also the land of the wolf as it had been almost since time began.

Grey wolf lived well in that land, never taking more than he needed to live and so often in his nomadic way left no trace behind. Though Grey Wolf must make a kill on occasion he took only meat and not spirit from the wilderness sacrifice. Grey Wolf knew that one day his spirit would move on and his body return to the earth whence it came and then new grass would grow over his bones and feed the forest deer and rabbit in the infinite cycle of life; this is the way of the universe.

One day three fat pigs came that way in their 4x4, 6 litre Guzzler Turbo SS. They stopped to take truffles from the forest, trampling over a sign that said, 'Please respect the forest; home to a diversity of wildlife Site of special scientific interest'. There

166

were at least seven trotter marks on the sign by the time they pushed their way past.

As they tore up the ground with scarcely a thought except for themselves they rooted out truffle upon truffle and scoffed them down with nary a taste bud affected by their passing.

One was heard to say, 'nice place this, I'm going to build a house here". Another said, 'I wonder who owns it?' and the third, with truffle stained drool running down his chest said, 'we do now.' Stuffed with truffles it didn't stop them opening the picnic basket they'd picked up earlier in a well known City store. They three were the Troffer brothers on their way to a small rural town bank, *Family Mutual*, which their own bank, Troffers & Lemmings Ltd, (limited to what they could get away with that is), had just taken over, they were looking forward so much to making a financial killing there and a few redundancies would soon wet their appetite for even more profit.

The Troffer brothers, Snot, Lardy and Dimbo, had made it good financially, although they remained unpopular with all who knew them, apart from a few self interested suckers up that hoped some spills from the gravy train might dribble their way.

Almost as though he had forgotten he'd already mentioned it, Snot Troffer exclaimed, 'Yup, this is it all right!'

'And what exactly is 'it'?' enquired Lardy.

'This is it. . . where I'm going to build my early retirement home, well more of a mansion I suppose, then I'll live here rooting out truffles for fun,' said Snot.

'Me too. . . Me too,' joined in Dimbo Troffer the youngest and most easily influenced of the three. They'd been orphans since they made their first windfall by selling their parents to a bacon factory. It had been Snot's idea but the brothers weren't far behind and were always willing henchmen to advantageous endeavours. Their new homes would be built with other's money, they knew just how to do that. . . that, after all, is how they made a living.

Family Mutual, despite pleas from the community for mercy, was in the event closed and the assets stripped for a tidy sum, even staff uniform had been recalled and sold for rags and any sitting tenants had moved out voluntarily after some comforting advice by heavies in balaclavas one night. . . the Troffers knew a trick or two about making money. The cash they made was split into three. . . that is three unequal lots; 'What Dimbo doesn't know won't hurt him I say, Lardy,' grinned Snot as he also hoodwinked the watching Lardy out of part of his share too.

Building started almost right away, no need for planning as no one would know and if they did the Troffers didn't know what 'lose' meant. . . unless it was happening to someone else.

Young Dimbo made his house from straw; it was easy to build and above all else was very cheap; it was warm, kept the rain out and had a couple of windows and a straw door at the front overlooking the path into the valley. Not far away, to his right was a pathway through a tangled mess of builder's rubble and felled tree debris to brother Lardy's house. Lardy had built with wood; more expensive than straw, but then he had accumulated a few extras over the years and felt that he was worth it. Lardy's house was on two floors and although he had a bedroom upstairs he mostly slept in the kitchen and used the upstairs room to keep an eye on his brothers' truffling expeditions. Lardy had many windows as this reduced the cost of the wood needed and to save further he had used plastic 'mock brass' fittings on the doors instead of the real thing. . . he felt safe enough there, I mean, why shouldn't he? To the right of Lardy's house was a high electrified fence which marked the vast boundary of Snot Troffer's new and private estate. Thoughtful as he was, brother Snot had installed cameras and automated gates that he could control from his fine best brick mansion. Oak doors, double glazing, treble garage for his new Red Guzzler 4x4 and his automated lawn mower, stone tile roof from the best quarries, polished and carved fine marble from the sweat shops of the orient, finest hardwoods from rain-forests, once upon a time the home of Jaguars and Orangutans, it was all there. . . it used to be somewhere else, but now it was all there. . . and all his.

There was a huge oil tank, complete with leak, as he never finished paying the plumber, in fact he never ever paid the whole bill, he just made them a token payment over which they were forced by circumstance and poverty to accept. Anyway, the oil was running down hill away from his place. The big diesel generator was housed in a remote building soundproofed with the last surviving Spanish Cork and to finish off his luxury a satellite mast projected above the lopped trees just over his fence near the rubbish tip where polystyrene and plastic lived on where all else had died.

Down stream of Troffer's new paradise the old one was dead or dying. The water tasted foul and eddies of oily scum danced the dance of death in the pools. No plants grew, no fish swam and the bank vegetation took on a mouldy yellow hue; the voles had long since left.

As Grey Wolf explored his ritual hunting ground his senses were affronted by the scattering of dead rabbits, all with tyre marks across their strewn bodies.

The constant humming noise of the electric fence assaulted his ears, 'no doubt why there are no deer,' he'd thought.

Grey Wolf was confused, it was like he'd stumbled upon another Earth. . . one he did not recognise.

Grey Wolf became aware of the straw house and for a moment thought he saw movement; he would go and ask what had happened to this beautiful land while he was away. He loped purposefully up the path from the valley.

At that precise moment in time, Dimbo vacantly stared out of his window with private thoughts about the bad things they had done to others. How many they had made homeless, jobless and joyless in their financial ventures. A glimmer of guilt slithered across his conscience. Then guilt rapidly turned to fear as Dimbo spotted Grey Wolf at a quick lope coming his way.

Startled, unable to think, Dimbo's staring, blind-panic piggy eyes scoured his little house of stolen straw for somewhere to hide. Was this the divine vengeance he always feared might hunt him down, was this the last he'd see of life, what would happen to all his investments. . . ? there was no where to go; he ran backwards and forwards and round and round in panic, then panic overtook his brain and he tore straight through his flimsy straw walls and bolted brainlessly to big brother Lardy's house, into which he burst with incoherent squeals.

Dimbo met Lardy head on as Lardy came down stairs to investigate. 'Wolf, Wolf, Wolf,' screamed Dimbo, 'lock your doors for pity's sake.' *(Probably the first time that the word pity had meant anything to him).*

Lardy knew full well that his cheap doors, obtained at a knock down price, couldn't lock and even if they did they wouldn't keep out a rabid, evil, pig-slaughtering wolf for long.

Knocking Dimbo out of the way so as to be able to go first, (an old motto of his springing to mind. . . *'devil take the hindmost')*, Lardy was out of the door and on his way to Snot's before Dimbo was even back on his feet.

'Oh, Great Sus of the underworld,' thought Lardy as he stopped dead, (a word the poignancy of which wasn't lost on him), at the closed electrified gates.

Dimbo caught Lardy up and nearly bowled him into the humming wires. Lardy teetered forward on the brink of extinction but fortune smiled upon them as the gate swung open and the speaker blared out Snot's commands, 'quick, Dopeys, inside the gate.' No invitation was ever so timely or welcome and none so quickly accepted.

Dimbo and Lardy were soon calming down in the safety of the secure brick mansion, with its bullet proof glass, nuclear fallout basement, and direct secure lines to the emergency services - always easy to arrange when you hold someone's mortgage in your gift.

From an upper window, guilt, fear and cowardice quickly forgotten, they now looked down sneeringly at Grey Wolf, who was still bemused by the entire arrangement. He was still curious and hoped to find answers from the people who seemed to be living there now.

Grey Wolf was having a bit of a huff and a puff by the time he'd reached the gate, as he was getting on a bit.

'Watch this,' said Snot as he opened the gate to admit their canine nemesis to his garden, much to the agitated concern of

Lardy and Dimbo. Grey Wolf stepped forward with a sense of gratitude that he had been admitted, now perhaps he would discover the truth. . . and indeed he would, indeed he would.

Once inside the gates they sneaked closed behind him. Snot Troffer gloated with overzealous glee as his trap was sprung. 'Money for old rope,' he cackled under his breath, 'candy from a baby,' which was something he was already familiar with doing anyway.

'Pray,' beseeched an out of his depth Grey Wolf, 'what has happened here to this beautiful land?'

'We'll be asking the questions,' said Snot. . .

'And giving the orders too,' sneered the now brave Dimbo.

Snot Troffer continued, 'You, sad old creature, are a trespasser, you have entered our very own private property uninvited and certainly most unwelcome. I'll have you know we could have you shot for this, and may still do so.'

Grey Wolf was much stronger than the three pigs put together, he knew his cause was just, he knew that the Troffers were weak on wisdom and that their cruelty was unjustifiable. . . but he was also wise enough to see that he stood alone against a tyranny beyond his means to counter.

Grey Wolf tried to appeal to their better side, not realising even their better side was still appalling.

'I only want to be free,' he said, 'just free in the land I love, free to endure until time commands my spirit joins the immortals that roam this earth. . . '

Cheered on by the now fearless Dimbo and Lardy, Snot Troffer looked down on his cornered and defenceless victim and called out, 'You'll be free alright. . . you won't cost us a penny, and as for immortality you might well find that sooner than you think - stuffed and exhibited in the foyer of Troffer for Lemmings head office.

The Troffers had full planning permission granted retrospectively, they were completely exonerated from any charges over the killing of Grey Wolf, who they said they'd found dead out in the woods somewhere. . . probably been killing some honest farmer's sheep or chickens and they became more and more rich in gold but poorer by the day in spirit. Dimbo and Lardy still twitched with a spasm of fear as they passed by the immortal and stuffed Grey Wolf in the front lobby of their Head Office.

The spirit of Grey Wolf would ever hold them in fear... their own fear. . : something deep in their psyche told them he was still out there somewhere.

No one escapes forever.

**

'For one who has conquered the mind, the mind is the best of friends; but for one who has failed to do so, his very mind will be his greatest enemy.' Bhagavad-Gita

**

172

33

Is this the truth about the Billy Goats Gruff Family?

This story is based on the Norwegian Folk Tale of three brother goats, the Gruff brothers, who sought pastures green on the other side of the river. The only bridge was controlled by a supposedly wicked Troll. The first two goats to cross were allowed to pass unmolested, they had each betrayed their elder brother who they said would be along shortly; and true enough he was and he beat the Troll and continued to join his younger brothers. (We can only assume they kept it a secret how they managed to cross the bridge unharmed). I can see some interesting latent messages in this story, especially for Trolls. I suggest we revisit this tale and see what the truth might have been.

The author recommends that those of a nervous disposition, the squeamish, vegans and goat herders find something else to read. You have been warned.

It was a fine summer's day, and the three Billy Goats Gruff were out doing what they did best. . . eating. They didn't care that much what they ate, they'd been up trees for apples, had the bark off saplings, and once, a camper woke to discover his only washed and drying underwear had disappeared off the line outside his tent.

In fact, the three goats, Little-Gruff, Middle-Gruff and Big-Gruff had virtually scoffed their way through most of the west side of the river that ran through the valley.

They had many times observed the lush grasses on the other side waving an inviting welcome to them in the summer breeze . . . but the river kept them from accepting.

'Let's find a way across to that lovely grub over there,' said Middle-Gruff. The other two, salivating drool down their beards, agreed at once. Big-Gruff, who was verging on being the sensible one, said, 'OK, we'll travel the bank upstream looking for a good crossing place. . . we'll go today. . . but we must stick together, for don't you remember our parents warning us never to cross the river? Remember? Just before they disappeared?'

The three brothers in hooves sauntered the upstream bank, occasionally stopping to browse on thistle and gawp salivating at the lush field that would soon be theirs, all theirs, a place to die for, such paradise as it looked. No conscious thought crossed their minds as to why there were no other animals out there feasting on such plenty.

It wasn't long before Little-Gruff was well out in front, he was a 'gobby little know it all,' couldn't be told a thing by his elder brothers. 'I know that,' he would bleat in the face of advice, 'do you think I'm stupid,' as his brothers tried to teach him something … and even then it wasn't much of a something.

'Stay in sight Little-gruff,' shouted Big-Gruff through a mouthful of nettles, 'do not cross the river without us!' Middle-Gruff shook his coat of the nettle flavoured spit that he'd just been sprayed with and passed wind. Big-Gruff thought he heard a reply in the breeze, 'yeah, yeah, yeah, dopey,' but he wasn't too sure as the sound of salivated nettle shoots chomping around in his mouth had obliterated much of his hearing – except for the chomping that is.

Middle-Gruff was chomping well too and had been since waking for breakfast and yet, all the while, his mind was on the field; His field, full of his grass, and as he dreamed he dreamed a horrific image. In his mind he saw Little-Gruff was there first, and eating, eating his grass in his field. 'Er, Big-Gruff, I think I'd better catch up with dear Little-Gruff. . . you know. . . make sure the poor little chap is ok and doesn't cross the river to my field. . . I mean our field, without us. I'll, er, just move ahead a bit quicker, OK?' Without awaiting reply, Middle-Gruff, seething with envy and filled with fermenting nettle leaves walked on briskly, without ever looking back to his big brother.

'Good chap, well done,' said Big-Gruff spotting a succulent bed of watercress, which was now all his, and his alone. Big-Gruff sent up a silent prayer for the find to the great Capricorn, Patron Saint of goats, who some say resided in an eternal-summer land filled with everlasting harvests.

Big-Gruff sauntered, chomped and salivated; Middle-Gruff ran, seethed and passed wind; but Little-Gruff was far away and had happened across something rather interesting. . . half hidden by dense foliage. . . a bridge! More importantly it was a bridge and pathway to his field and his grass.

With eyes only on his field across the river and not a single thought for his brothers or his missing parent's warnings Little-Gruff was off, the bridge's wooden boards clonking to the sound of his little hooves, 'trip trap trip trap trip tra. . .'

Horror of all horrors, something from the world of a goat's worst nightnannies leapt over the railings and stood hunched and threatening in front of him. . . It was a Troll.

'Who's that crossing my bridge?' demanded the Troll, and some would say he was quite within his Troll rights to ask.

'Gulp, it's only little me, Little-Gruff,' quaked the trembling Little-Gruff, babying himself in the hope of sympathy. 'Please don't eat me, I am thin and starving. . . I only want to go and eat in my field .... I mean that field, if you let me go my bigger brother will be along soon and he is much fatter than I, you could eat him instead.' Some thoughts crossed the Troll's mind, a rare experience, but it occurred to the Troll, that firstly, that field was his, secondly he too was starving and thirdly, he hadn't eaten a goat in months. That was enough thinking for the day.

Little-Gruff looked at the grass, his grass; the Troll looked at the goat, his goat, and before Little-Gruff could move or call for help the Troll was on him; mercifully a swift death; with the goat's limp body under his arm the Troll swung his body over the rail and under the bridge. There, up on a dry bank in the shelter of the bridge and hidden by undergrowth, the Troll sat comfortably surrounded by a scattered bone collection, a hobby of some years now, and he tucked in to the tastiest freshest goat he'd had in ages.

Only half way through his dinner he heard another customer arriving, a trifle annoyed by the disturbance at mealtime he felt he must respond to anything crossing his bridge. His bridge, did you ask? Yes, his bridge; a Troll bridge, built by the Troll, for the Troll, it was the Troll that built it and maintained it, not the government, not the council, but old Trolley boy himself, and hard work it had been at times too. 'Trip. . . Trap. . . Trip . . . Trap' came the heavier hooves of Middle-Gruff, rushing to catch up and be with his little brother. . . he was almost across too when with great power and speed the troll vaulted the railings to confront his latest 'customer'.

'And who is this that crosses me bridge,' demanded the Troll, never having been one much for grammar, as he'd left school early to take up a trade.

Middle-Gruff was made of the same stuff as his younger brother, only his stuff was older and bigger. 'Ah, mister Troll Sir, tis only I, Middle-Gruff. . . if you'd just let me pass by sir I can promise you a much bigger goat is coming this way as we speak.'

Middle-Gruff was sure that the Troll's eyes looked away for a moment as if to see if a bigger goat was indeed close by, it was his chance to make a run for it back to his now beloved Big-Gruff brother. Too late and too slow, Middle-Gruff's first twitch was his last twitch and soon he joined his younger brother under the bridge. The Troll finished his first course and without a break, nor drink of water, and with only a belch between them, went straight on with the second course. The Troll hadn't eaten so well in years, 'Lovely grub,' he thought, using a fine rib bone to pick bits of meat from between his teeth, 'mmm lovely grub.'

Above him the Troll heard a heavy clatter on his wooden boards, 'TRIP TRAP TRIP TRAP'. What a busy day it had been, what with all the exertion, dealing with two awkward customers and being stuffed by that huge dinner he was drowsy and could hardly move any way. The Troll settled back with hands on belly and afternoon napped.

Above the bridge, above the Troll, and above the dismembered bodies of his brothers, mum, dad and several other relatives, Big-Gruff was blissfully unaware. Trip trapping his heavy hooves across the wood enjoying the sound it made and bathed in glorious late afternoon sunshine he eyed the lush grass in his new field. Big-Gruff looked around for his brothers but couldn't see them, sure that they had found the bridge and crossed over, he assumed that they had been at a good dinner and were now resting somewhere out of sight. 'I'll eat first,' Big-Gruff said to himself, an old habit, 'then I'll join my brothers later.' Big-Gruff stuffed himself silly with the sweetest, lushest grass he'd ever encountered, until he could hardly move. 'Lovely grub,' he thought trying to tongue an awkward bit of leaf from between his teeth, 'mmm, lovely grub.' As evening approached and night's dusk put out the lights Big-Gruff settled down comfortably in some long grasses that sheltered him from the night breeze of the valley.

'What a good day,' thought Big-Gruff, 'what a good day,' then just as he closed his eyes to sleep he thought he heard something move nearby. . . and. . . as night fell upon him. . . so did the Troll.

'What a good day,' thought the Troll, 'what a good day,' as Big-Gruff's lifeless body was dragged off to join his brothers.

Well, there we have it, one version of The three Billy Goats Gruff; food for thought eh?

In the original, the two younger goats, so quick to betray their siblings, were let go across by the Troll. . . trusting old Troll eh? Then that vicious bad tempered big Billy goat Gruff turns up and in an unprovoked frenzy murders the Troll, who is only asking the question, 'who's that crossing my bridge?' It was murder right enough but Big Billy Goat Gruff could have got off with trollslaughter due to diminished common sense and only done twenty hours community service no doubt.

The murdered Troll would have left behind a number of grieving dependants who had to move out of the area because Big Billy Goat Gruff was still free. It would not be long before the bridge fell in to disrepair for want of maintenance and the council would refuse to do it as it had never been adopted. The valley would thereafter always be divided. Nothing would be reported in the papers and no memorial to the Troll ever erected. The courts, headed by Sir Hugh Wilberforce Gruff would make sure of that.

**

'Change the way you look at things
and the things you look at will change.'

**

34

Value added. . ?

It started with some seed, picked freely by dear Mrs Good-grace, from a Hollyhock that overhung a public path. Lovingly collected and placed safely into a folded envelope the seeds were carried back home along with their new owner's benevolent dreams. . . then forgotten, misplaced in the shed for a year.

It was a pleasant surprise when the seeds turned up again, discovered by her helpful neighbour, Mr Kindly. 'Oh you can have them,' she said, 'I meant to plant them then forgot, pity, they'd have been lovely.'

They all germinated, part of God's nature, the way of the universe you know, there was no charge, the rain came and the seeds grew unhindered into fine plants nurtured by the Sun and a small pot of garden earth. 'Lovely, dear, but you have too many,' said his wife, Argusina Kindly, 'and I think they're just

a bit too tall for our little garden.'

'All right love,' he replied, 'I'll not waste them, I'll give them to Mr Grubitout at the nursery, I'm sure he'll find a good home for them.'

**

Not so far away, at the posh end of the village, Mr and Mrs Havalot were in the process of having their garden landscaped by Mr Trimmings and Sons and never having lifted a finger in the garden themselves, they were taking his advice. He should be good as they had seen his old pick-up outside the 'big house', owned by none other than *the* Lucre El Dorado, banking consultant.

He'd 'do a good job', Trimmings had said, and 'keep the price low for them as the Havalots were struggling to live on the rents from their Lucerne holiday flats, and what with the mooring costs at the yacht club too.'

**

'Just the very thing for you, Trimmings,' said Grubitout at the nursery sales counter, 'some fine Hollyhocks, mixed colours and only £6 a plant, I tell you what, I'll discount them at £5.50 for you, can't say fairer than that, a real steal as they say.'

'I'll take the lot, Grubitout,' replied Trimmings, eyeing the strong dark green foliage and beginnings of good stems – they'd flower this year with luck.

'Right, that's 20 plants at £5.50, er um, £110 plus VAT at 20%. . . dreadfully sorry about that, can't be escaped you know, we all have to pay. . . so that will be £132 if you please,' said Grubitout not so much organically but more orgasmically as he rung the bell on the nursery till.

**

'All planted Mrs Havalot – I got you some real beauties, nursery grown, quality plants from Mr Grubitout's Establishment. . . Let's see now. . . that's £150 for the plants, real beauties, mixed colours he said, you won't find better anywhere I dare say. . . then only £50 labour, tell you what, you're nice people, make that just £45, as I like you. . . £150 plus £45 is er £195, plus that damned VAT at 20%. . the scourge of the nation that, still, we all have to pay it, can't be escaped. . . so that comes to £233 then please. Thanks for your business, call me back any time,' smiled a very happy Mr Trimmings the landscaper.

Meanwhile out in the garden 20 free seedlings flourished in God's earth with free rain and free sunshine. Their added value would be the scented flowers that perfumed the garden, the drop-in pollen café for the bees, no charge, no tax, and later the seed heads would feed winter hungry birds, free, no tax, their autumn leaves would fall and enrich the soil for free, no tax. . . such is the way of nature.

Some years later, as the Hollyhocks developed, they began to spread and overhang a garden wall, there to be spotted by that dear little old lady Mrs Goodgrace out walking with her grand-daughter; She reached out and picked a few seeds. Carefully placing them in a folded envelope she said, 'I'll jolly well make sure I plant them this time, I bet they'll look lovely, come on, let's go home for tea and find some plant pots, I have some really pretty green ones I saved free from the rubbish tip.'

**

'Beware knowing the price of everything and the value of nothing.'
Oscar Wilde
**

Be not afraid of going slowly –
only of being still.
The Moon-gate beckons.

35

Rupert the Alaskan Malamute reports.

O ur undercover operator - an anonymous brown mongrel we suitably code-named 'Buster' - posing as an ordinary family pet infiltrated this awful organisation. This is what Buster sniffed out.

Turn an old dog into a goldmine in one easy move.
Read on then call us at P'ooch Power Therapies
Own a pet dog? Want to make some easy money?
No outlay. All advertising, appointments and accountancy carried out by our highly professional and ethical staff.
You simply receive a cheque in the post after each successful appointment.

Based on new science brought to our own cyber specialists by spirit messengers from far off Vulcania.
Now you can do your bit. . . and so can your dog.
Worried that your dog won't be up to the task?
Don't worry, full training is given on how to explain and interpret any anomalies.
As proof we publish a letter of thanks from just one of thousands of satisfied P'ooch Power clinicians.

'Dear p'ooch Power people, I was so worried that my old brown spaniel would be unsuitable but your training package has put my mind at rest. In fact the more odd his habits and the more dopey he looks the greater has been our success rate, with large numbers of referrals and repeat callers. We just can't believe our luck, I'm so happy with all those generous cheques you keep sending me. I'm thinking of getting another dopey looking dog so as to fit in more clients. Thank you so much for all your brilliant help. Yours, A M Greedy.'

How does it work you ask? Simple, you do not need to know anything, as before clients knock your door, they will already have been convinced by our psychiatric and NLP trained call centre staff based in Barkistarn. You won't need to answer awkward questions, just follow the guidelines we give you and your next cheque will be on its way.

The p'ooch power therapy creates an apparent cure for all ailments, whether physical or mental, because it allows the client's mind to go to a higher plane of consciousness and so their problem disappears. The effect may be temporary and a series of repeat treatments should always be recommended.

How to – a guide.

Welcome your client into your home, asking them not to speak unless absolutely necessary as your dog is meditating prior to treatment. This reduces the number of questions asked. Make them comfortable, we suggest a cup of tea and a cheap biscuit is sufficient.

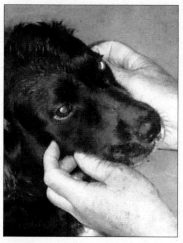
Bring in your dog in silence, some of our clinicians take their dogs for long walks and give them a big dinner before seeing a client as it makes the dog look quietly thoughtful, and certainly less boisterous, always recommended for dogs like Boxers. Place your dog directly in front of the client, preferably eyeball to eyeball but this is not essential. Tell the client that the dog knows best how to complete the therapy, even if it

appears to have fallen asleep. For full recovery the client must continue to believe.

Tell the client to place hands on the dog's head and to silently ask for answers to their problems, they should stare into the dog's eyes and repeat the word 'Vulcania' seven times with a breath between each word. If your dog is prone to unexpected bouts of biting, use a muzzle and explain that it acts like an aerial and aids communication.

A check sheet is included which allows you to interpret the dog's actions for the client.

We advise all our clinicians to be familiar with these standard interpretations.
(Canine Interpretations copyright P'ooch Power Therapies.)

<u>**What to say if your dog does this:-**</u>

Dog growls .... he's driving away evil spirits.
Dog barks ....he's calling upon higher beings for support.
Dog falls asleep .... he's gone into a deeper trance.
Dog leans forward ..... bringing the omega energy closer, a good sign.
Dog leans back ....client's energy is so good dog has to move away from the power
Dog belches or passes wind ..... this is the release of negative energy drawn from the client.
Dog licks client .... he's repairing a weak spot in the client's aura. . . they are very lucky as this usually costs extra.

<u>**What to say if the client does this:-**</u>
Client falls asleep - the effect of a truly powerful omega melding energy surge – a good sign
Client fidgets a lot - same as above.
Client complains that the dog smells - explain that increased sensory perception, like the sense of smell, is one of the prime

benefits. The client might find that the smell will linger for at least 48 hours. Repeat treatments are recommended.

Client complains that the dog was sucking energy out and not putting it in - Tiredness and a lack of energy are a good sign as it means their body and mind have been working hard during the therapy.

Client wants money back - explain that this invites bad Karma and may cause the dog to bite or pass on tics, fleas or other diseases. *(Full payment keeps the client protected.)*

Client wants to take the dog away or have private sessions

1. If your dog is knackered and looks like it will need a vet's bill soon, let them take the dog and purchase another dopey looker. You can save money by choosing from a dog's home. If the dog is useless at the therapy simply return it and chose another.

(A small donation from your own generous cheque will work wonders.)

2. If your dog is a good earner then explain that the dog is an expert in communicating with Vulcanian aliens who use it to channel messages. Removing the dog could cause irreparable harm. The bad energy could cause rabies to infect the new owner.

Client complains that no answers are coming from the dog. - offer a 10% discount on a reappointment and say you will get the dog to meditate more prior to the meld process next time.

Client says that they are overwhelmed by answers - ask the client to write it down and we will use as testimonials in our brochures. Explain that they must be very lucky and a special person indeed to exercise such a brilliant melding. If they have a dog themselves, see if you can sign them up and you receive 10% of all their treatment fees.

You'd be barking mad not to join us.
Success guaranteed.

P'ooch Power is part of the Natural Resource Exploitation Conglomerate , an International Group of Companies operating out of Luxuriborg.

Pooch Power Therapies are a not for profit registered charity and operate on a no win no fee basis. Terms and conditions apply.

Closing report from Rupert.

Our undercover agent Buster was retired after this highly dangerous mission and lived out the rest of his life peacefully in a guest house on the south coast. The dog abusing company was closed down as it happened by the Inland Revenue. If you are thinking of mind melding with dogs please be aware that some dogs will take over and control you. You'll have seen them in the parks making their so called owners throw things for them and lots more. You have been warned. Rupert Malamute.

**

*'They say, never look a gift horse in the mouth,
pity they didn't do that with the Trojan horse -
it would have saved them a lot of trouble.'*

**

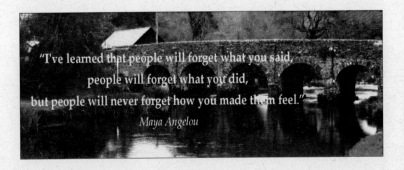

"I've learned that people will forget what you said, people will forget what you did, but people will never forget how you made them feel."

Maya Angelou

36

Uncle Robert's Magic Carpet.

Little Sophie was adamant; she was *not* going to stay with her great aunt and uncle for a whole two weeks while her mother was away on some silly training thing for work.

'But you'll love it there Sophie; I always did when I was young. Uncle Robert and Auntie Florence are really kind people and it's not for very long.'

Nothing seemed to change Sophie's mind, 'I'll stay here on my own then mum, and Mrs what's-er-name next door can keep an eye on me.'

'No Sophie. That won't do at all. You are far too young and Mrs Gracie is too old. Poor dear must be ninety. We must sort this out soon, today would be good as I have already written to them. Aunt and uncle live in the most wonderful old cabin up in the mountains, fresh air, good food, why, they even had horses when I was there, my favourite was a big friendly white one called. . . ' Sophie interrupted, 'Horses? They have horses? Will they let me ride them?'

Sophie's mum saw a glimmer of hope, this sudden change of mind was a blessing. 'Oh, I'm sure they will, and you can take their old dog for walks in the forest too,' she said keenly, hoping the dog might still be alive, after all, that was twenty years ago.

'I'll put you on the bus and give you a note for the driver to let you off at the right place and Aunt Florence will be waiting there for you.'

'Okay mum, but if there are no horses I'm coming home on the next bus.'

True to their word, the driver dropped Sophie off at a remote countryside bus stop and Aunt Florence was patiently waiting for her. Sophie liked her immediately. 'Isn't it quiet here Auntie. . . where is the car?'

'Ah, a car, yes, we had one of those contraptions a long time ago Sophie, but now we just look after ourselves up here in the mountains. Come along, give me your bag and we'll take a nice walk home through the woods. It's not far, about two miles, that's all.'

'Two miles!' thought Sophie, that's like forever. I don't even walk to school and that's only around the corner.'

The walk turned out to be very pleasant and not tiring at all as they walked on a carpet of soft pine needles and dry leaves. Sunshine lit the ground between the trees and in the distance a woodpecker could be heard making a home in some lucky tree. Squirrels, curious to see who was walking through their forest, popped their heads around branches to watch. By the time Sophie reached the cabin she was already looking for the next adventure.

As soon as he heard their happy chatter arriving, Uncle Robert stopped digging in the vegetable garden and waved wildly, so pleased he was to see them. 'Hello my dear Sophie. My, how you have grown, you must be ten years old by now. . .' Sophie interrupted, 'actually, I'm eleven now uncle, or will be next month.'

They went into the house and showed Sophie to her room, 'Your mum stayed in here too you know. She liked it because the window looks out over the paddock. We had lots of horses then.'

Sophie's heart dropped. No horses? 'Have you no horses now then auntie?' she enquired, hardly able to hide her disappointment.

'Just the one now dear, a great big friendly white horse called. . . ' Sophie interrupted again, 'I see him, I see him, there, by the fence looking this way. Do you think he knows I am here Aunt?'

Aunt Florence laughed, 'he sure will, once you feed him a carrot or two. Go with uncle while I prepare the dinner. Not too long now, you'll need to calm down before bed time. Not too long Robert and not too many carrots either!'

Over the next few days Sophie enjoyed the pleasures of the countryside. In between picking berries, helping in the kitchen and feeding the chickens, she played happily in the nearby woods. Instead of seeing animals on television she saw them for real and was always being amused by the squirrels that visited the gardens. But most of all, Sophie liked the friendly old horse. Sometimes Uncle Robert would sit her high up on his back, he seemed to like Sophie being there. He only walked slowly and never too far, for he was indeed very old now. Uncle Robert told Sophie not to become too fond of the old horse as he was likely to be going the same way as the others had, possibly while Sophie was staying at the cabin. Sophie wasn't quite sure what to make of this but every morning when she woke; the old horse was peering at her window from the paddock. Perhaps dreaming of when he was young or perhaps just waiting patiently for another carrot.

Sophie's next favourite thing was sitting on the colourful rug in front of the log fire after supper, when aunt and uncle would tell her stories, stories about her mum, life in the mountains and their travels when they were younger. One night Uncle Robert was to tell Sophie about the carpet she loved to sit on, it was a magic carpet. 'Well so the old gentleman told us when we bought it in a market place in the ancient city of Thebes,' confided Uncle Robert, with a glance towards the window to make sure no one else was there. 'We made instant friends with the shopkeeper. Mustapha Mohamed was his name. It was the only magic carpet he had ever seen in his entire life but he'd not been able to find the secret which made it work. He said that it would be up to us to find the key that unlocked the magic.'

Sophie was spellbound, 'Have you tried abracadabra? Or open sesame? She asked, watching the rug very carefully as she spoke.

Her aunt Florence laughed, yes dear, we've tried them all and in the end we gave up. We only have Mustapha's word that it is a magic carpet and whether it is or is not, we've had it so long

189

now it's become part of the family. See, it still has all the bright colours and there are no holes in it anywhere, it's just like when we first had it.'

Evenings could be cold in the mountains and snow was always expected at this time of year. Tonight could be the night. 'Well, time for bed Sophie but before you go I have some sad news about your old friend out in the paddock. We are not wealthy people Sophie and the time has come to send our old horse to another place. Possibly a man may arrive tomorrow to collect him.'

Sophie was very upset as she went to bed; she wished her mum was there, she would know what to do. Even though it was very late, Sophie was still wide awake when she heard her aunt and uncle go to bed. They were soon snoring happily. Sophie looked out of her window, the snow had stopped and by the light of a full moon Sophie could see the old horse looking at her from over his fence. She saw him shiver with cold and shake off a little snow from his mane. She must do something; she could not rest until she had. Then Sophie had a wonderful idea. Tiptoeing in bare feet, she crept through the house and picked up the carpet from in front of the fire, how warm and dry it felt. Still in bare feet she crossed the snowy ground to the paddock and managed to climb onto the fence with the carpet in her arms. It was cold outside but nothing was going to stop such a kind deed for this beloved animal. The feeble old horse moved shivering alongside the fence as though knowing he was about to have a warm coat. Soon the carpet was comforting him across his back. Little did Sophie realise that the key to the magic carpet was not in words at all but in actions of unselfish kindness. After all these years the carpet began to work its magic again, the old white horse was changing before Sophie's eyes, becoming more white, taller and muscles began to cover his old bones. He was young again, young, strong and no longer cold. But more! He was no longer just an old horse but a splendid unicorn! Sophie watched in amazement as the unicorn shook off the carpet, took two steps forward and rose into the air, it was flying, flying over the paddock fence and away into the distant moonlit mountains. Sophie gathered the magic carpet in her arms, brushed the snow off and returned it to the warm fire place where it would dry off overnight. Sophie didn't feel the cold any more and was soon in bed and fast asleep.

Sophie was still snugly asleep when she was suddenly woken by shouting outside her window. It was Uncle Robert, he had discovered the old horse was missing, 'Florence, Florence, the horse has gone, come quick, look!'

Sophie quickly dressed in warm clothes and rushed outside to join them.

'Well I never Florence. That old horse could never jump this fence and the gate is still locked.'

'That's not all Robert, look, there are no hoof prints in the snow outside the paddock. How could he possibly have got out? The man was coming to collect him today too, what on earth can we say to him?'

Sophie wasn't sure if it had all been a dream but she chose to tell what she knew anyway, 'He just turned into a unicorn and flew across the mountains over that way,' she said pointing excitedly.

Aunt Florence gently brushed her hand over Sophie's hair, 'Bless you my dear child, what a lovely idea.'

'Yes,' said Uncle Robert, 'what an imagination they have eh? Well, it's a mystery to me. Let's have breakfast and see if we can find out how he escaped later.'

They never did find out. Only Sophie knew. . . and now you of course.

**
'If you believe in me, I'll believe in you.'
**

37

The Joy of Cycling.

Narwhal Bliss OBE was in his late fifties and had retired early on a banker's pension. Worn out by the pressures of a luxurious city life he had moved with his wife to rural Devon, a land of hills, trees and narrow lanes. He'd also taken up cycling. A state of the art racing bicycle and embarrassingly tight fitting and wasp like yellow and black racing lycra outfit had set him back about three and a half thousand pounds. Fortunately he couldn't be recognised when wearing his helmet, goggles and gossamer silk pollen-filtering scarf. This was the only reason his wife let him out. Lucinda found it an abhorrent almost disgusting sight and sought solace in gin and cream tea sessions at the country club with her friends. All had similar stories to tell.

It was 11.45 Friday morning and Narwhal Bliss was out for a ride, not too far, perhaps twelve miles or so. He chose the narrow coastal road for its fine woodlands, its twisting, bend filled treasures, high hedges and pretty flowers that leaned out across the tarmac. As he wobbled along slowly he felt the gentle breeze pass by, his helmet camera recording everything so he could play it back to his wife in the evening and his ears and mind filled with the sound of taped whale music. Bliss by name and Bliss was what he was having. The road was his, not a soul in sight, except for an occasional vehicle travelling in the opposite direction. Some of them seemed to wave at him – he smiled and nodded back. How foolish people were, not to be out enjoying the countryside and this fine weather, still, it meant the road was his, all his.

Five yards behind the euphoric Narwhal, an old Devon farmer sat patiently in crawler gear listening to his catch-up box set of The Archers, a few yards behind him was the full muck spreading bowser he was towing. At least a hundred vehicles had now joined the procession. Some would gladly have turned around and aborted their journey. This was not such a road. About half way back, a policeman had time to leave his car and book a woman for using her mobile phone. The fact that she was a midwife trying to organise alternative assistance for an imminent home birth, cut no ice with the policeman, whose bladder was likely to rupture if he didn't get relief soon. Two cars behind them and Bob Lovalot realised he would never get his girlfriend home before her husband was back from morning rugby training and he was already in trouble with his own wife for not remembering something she thought he should have – whatever it was. Life looked like a change was in the wind. Also in the wind, was the rich farmyard aroma from the muck spreader aided by the fact it had sprung a leak. Two children on their way to school after a doctor's appointment threw up out of the back windows of a brand new Audi, their mother's screams clearly audible above the hooting of horns, abuse and engine revvings.

'Oooooeeeeooooowww, oooieeow' howled Narwhal as he sang along with the whale tape. He thought about stopping in a small and very rare lay-by but changed his mind at the last minute; after all, what was the point on such a fine day. He ped-alled a little harder to see if he could catch up with a squirrel that was sitting on the road up ahead, peacefully scratching an ear with its foot. Narwhal glanced down at the electronic device on the handlebars, he didn't understand any of it, except the speed and that was in some foreign thing, not miles per hour, ah, eight, excellent, he was doing eight somethings. This pleased him, eight was nice number. He turned up the volume of his whale music, smiled and thought deeply about the num-ber eight. How beautiful it was, its sound, its shape, its mathe-matical importance, chess boards have them, two to the power of three was eight. Though he wasn't completely sure about that as banking wasn't about maths as far as he remembered. Still eight was a lovely number.

Far behind him was a different sort of eight, in fact it sounded similar but began with an 'H'. Nobody could overtake safely, too risky with the tractor and trailer taking up so much room, even a deranged youth on fizzy drinks and driving his dad's Subaru decided it was a move too far.

Somewhere in a nearby town a judge was signing the arrest warrant for a young man stuck in car 74 and who had set off early so as not to miss his court appearance. An irate home owner was phoning around for another plumber and no, he didn't care what it cost, as long as the blighter turned up on time. A dog had been left in the house too long, desperate to get out, it had urinated profusely on the best carpet and taken out its frustrations on the antique chair legs, splinters costing about fifty quid a time mixed with a rabid saliva as the pet took its revenge. The dog's oblivious owner turned to her friend in car 53 and said, 'oh dear, little Flufkins will be waiting for me, probably sitting by the door waiting patiently for his mummy to come home.' Her friend, who was a cat lover anyway, simply drawled a long expressionless 'yeees', and stared out of the window at the unmoving scenery.

Narwhal's mind began to roam to food. He'd recently read about a muscle building bean curd and marmite sandwich in his cycling magazine, 'Cycling Supremos, magazine for the gifted elite', time to cycle back and try it out. With only half an unsighted glance behind him, Narwhal briefly flicked out his right arm, grabbed the bars again and slowly wobbled around to face his journey home.

His goggles were slightly steamed and in any event his spectacles couldn't be worn at the same time, so they weren't. He could see well enough for his own needs and was now amazed at the number of vehicles out on the road since he'd started out, how glad he was that he was turning for home. He certainly wouldn't want to get caught up in that traffic. The stench of overheating cars, diesel, petrol and some awful smell he'd never experienced in the City affronted his nostrils. Thank God he'd got a bike. As he passed by the now mostly stationary collection of motor vehicles he smiled and nodded back at those who seemed to be waving at him. 'Ah,' he thought, blessed are the cyclists, for they shall inherit the roads. See how loved we are.'

Narwhal waved, smiled and wobbled his way home, passing motorists exchanging accident details, motorists calling the AA for help, motorists in open war with their neighbours, partners, wives, children and a happy looking policeman watching from the other side of a hedge.

Narwhal switched on his second favourite cycling tape, 'Zoo animals in slumber', and to the sound of a snoring Galapagos tortoise, he dreamed of his sandwich and blissfully pedalled home.

Where would he go tomorrow?

*No cyclists, squirrels nor any other living
creatures were harmed in the making of this story.*

38

Nice man with a mission.

'Les,' she said tentatively, as she handed her husband a cup of tea over his newspaper, 'one of the curtain rail brackets seems to be broken.'

'Yes', he replied, 'I know, it had a slight crack in it when I fitted it, but I just haven't had a moment to myself to fix it. I've got to pop in to town and buy some guttering bits for the shed. I'll sort the curtain rail then', he said, thinking through lots of other jobs too.

He'd finished his tea and as she took away his cup asked if he was mowing the lawn that day as the weather forecast was looking good.

'Lawn? Lawn? Curtain rail? Can't do everything you know, what do you want. . . the lawn or the curtain rail?' he replied, remembering an old saying about brooms and backsides. Les looked at the clock and stood up.

'Well the curtain rail would be good before it breaks all together, and your family are coming for tea tomorrow evening. which reminds me, I must get on and bake some cakes.'

His morning tea and Branflakes under his belt he shoehorned his clean black shoes on to his neatly socked feet. Unlocking the front door with a neatly organised bunch of keys, and before stepping into the street he turned and called out, 'Perhaps you'd like me to re paint the outside of the house and fit new carpets before tea time too.'

'No, no need for that.' she called back as she fed the dog. 'Don't be long. . . drive carefully. . . see you soon.' She was used to his little ways.

Jane, that's Les' lovely and long suffering wife, wondered what time he'd be back, he'd got form. Les had a compulsive habit of helping people; a need to serve, assist, guide, mentor and give altruistically of self for others. 'I wonder if he'll be back for tea,' she thought, her eyes dwelling on the long green grass of their lawn, growing even longer in the sunshine.

Lunch time came and went and no sign of Les, then the phone rang. 'Oh, hello,' said a woman's voice, 'can I speak to Les?'

'He's not back from town yet, shall I get him to call you when he comes in?' Jane was interrupted by a 'No', 'I'll call back later, it's about my lawn, he said he'd cut it for me. . . and it's such a nice day today. . . I'll phone again, bye.'

Jane had only just put the phone down when it rang once more. 'hello,' she said, hoping it was Les reporting in on his day. . . but it wasn't.

'Hello, is that Les' wife? He's just called by and re wired a cooker socket for me. . . and he'd looked in the loft for me for an old pair of comfortable slippers I'd lost. . . I've had them for years you know, couldn't be without them, not sure I remember much these days anyway. . . where was I? Ah yes, are you phoning about the council tax rebate?'

'No,' said Jane. 'Yyou called me about my husband Les.'

'Did I? Ah yes, that's right. . . he's left his glasses here. . . well I think the're his. . . can't see too clearly as I've mislaid my own. Perhaps when he calls by he could run the mower over my lawn, it's such a nice day for it.'

Tea time came and went and still the phone was silent. Then, just as Jane finished off an out of date reduced carton of yoghurt for her tea, the phone rang. Above the sound of her excited dogs she could hear it was Les. 'Sorry dear, tried to phone, couldn't get a signal up on the moors'.

'Moors?' Jane queried in her 'let's have no more nonsense' voice.

'Yes dear, moors. I was on my way back to find my glasses when I stopped for a hitch hiker, poor old chap, retired on ill health from the Army, trying to get home he was. He had no money either, he didn't. Well, by the time I'd gone to the cash point to take some money out for him, then driven up past Newton-le-willows'....... ' and where the devil is that?' interjected an irate and exasperated wifely voice.... 'Cheshire, dear, near Merseyside', replied Les, 'nice part of the world, you should see it sometime, any way, he'd been away for a while, somewhere in the Caribbean I think, and his lawn needs cutting. I've said I'll do it for him but his mower needs a service. Anyway, to cut a long story short, I asked around for a mower and his neighbour, a nice old lady called Mavis ... her husband flew Lancasters in the war you know, ..' 'Here it comes', thought Jane. ..... Les continued in full enthusiastic flow, 'she asked if, as I was borrowing her mower, I could cut her lawn too. Can't talk too long as I'm just sitting down to one of Mavis' cheese ... nice cheddar .. salads, then I'll get started. Don't wait up - I may be gone for some time.'

Jane thought, 'didn't some famous person say that before ... ah yes, Scot's doomed polar expedition ... Captain Oates ... just before he died.'

Les continued, 'I'll try and phone before I set off home dear.' The line went dead and silence ruled.

The night came and went, Jane was up early, had breakfast and fed the dogs.

The phone rang, 'that'll be your master,' she told the dogs as she walked to the phone. 'hello?' she said picking it up to her ear.

'It's me dear,' said a tired voice that had only half slept all night on a sofa with an old Rotweiller and a scurvy parrot for company. I may not get back until tea time, I'm picking up a prescription for an old lady who lives a couple of doors away, the chemist won't be open until nine.'

'A couple of doors away from where, Les?' she asked patiently. She heard him ask someone in the background where he was .... she heard a muffled voice say, 'Pankhurst Alms Houses in .... unintelligible ...... County Durham.' 'It's ok Les, I heard it', thinking better of asking what the hell he thought he was doing there, 'see you when you get home.'

Jane missed his next call about lunchtime as she was outside unsuccessfully trying to wrestle a reluctant lawnmower from its comfy resting place in Les' shed.

Jane later picked up the voice mail message, Les was moving steadily southwards; three lawns and a prescription to his credit and a job offer from age concern in Liverpool rejected, he'd been to the bank machine yet again as he'd met another tramp.

Only God knows what other jobs he did or people he helped before staggering in with a half eaten Indian takeaway, about seven in the evening.

He slumped on the sofa, two dogs on his lap, his eyes closed and his mouth dropped open.

Jane sat next to him watching a pre recorded programme about piped drainage systems in Canada in high definition and surround sound. She couldn't turn it off as it was on auto cue for Les' favourite programmes and he'd put the controls somewhere.

Sitting in a comfy chair across the room with head slumped forward at the same angle as the empty tea cup hanging on her finger, an old lady called Mavis snored in unison with Les, that nice man on a mission.

The phone rang, the dogs barked, Les Grunted, Mavis twitched in her new home and Jane got up to answer, ...'hello?'

'Sorry to trouble you, but can you tell Les there's no need to cut my lawn now as some nice men came by earlier and only charged me £70, tell Les I'm so sorry as I know how much he always enjoys doing it.'

**

'The present time is the only time over which we have dominion. The most important person is always the person with whom we are, who is right before us, for who knows if we will have dealings with any other person in the future. The most important pursuit is making that person happy for that alone is the pursuit of life.'

Tolstoy
**

39

Publishing a Biography.
(Eavesdropping a meeting between a publisher and author.)

'Well I've read your manuscript – not bad – needs a bit of tidying - some sentences too wordy and some appalling grammar. Mavis, our tame editor and a cross between Dickens and an Orang-utan with typing skills, will knock it into shape for you. We'll deduct her wages out of yours. Easy done, our accounts people are real wizards, ex-tax office folk.

Smiling inanely, 'Thank you, I didn't realise how easy it was to be published with such a reputable company.'

'Whoa, don't jump the gun, hold your horses a bit, the chickens haven't hatched yet. The story is good, well, alright, workable. However, the biography bit is complete tosh. For starters, what made you pick such a stupid name?'

Surprised, 'But, that *is* my name. I just wrote the truth.'

'Truth? Truth? For God's sake, they don't want the truth. They want gossip, intrigue, mystery, heroes and above all an author they can believe in, a real someone – you know, like a soap actor or a convicted politician. Let's sort your bio out while I have you in the office.'

With that, Montague Falcon de Chevalier took out his old Woolworth's biro and began to write. 'What about, *Sherpa Cameron*, illegitimate son of an Earl and a Tibetan peasant. That has a nice ring to it.'

'No, I don't think that would be right at all,' the author replied, still somewhat shocked at a top publisher not wanting the truth.

'Okay, okay, what about Peregrine Gainsborough, descendant of the famous painter, your parents are Cornish farmers related to Tess of the Durbavilles.'

Verging on indignant, 'No, no, I couldn't be party to that. . .'

Brutally interrupting, 'If you want that book seen in the light of day and read by anyone other than you and your mother you're going to have to start listening to me.' With that, an irate Montague threw a few new books on the desk. 'Look,' he said, pointing a stubby finger at each cover in turn, 'Sexual secrets of Freemasonry, by Babs Malone – the inside story by the wife of a leading mason who was accidentally killed during a frenzied ritual, they reckon that to produce such depraved and graphic detail she must have been present. There were surprisingly no prosecutions. Or this – Games in the Second House, an exposé by Lord Butterfield, real name John Smith from a council estate in Islington. Or this – 'Sir Edmund Hilary – Nazi Spy, by Abraham Goldsmith, real name Bob Jones a failed trade unionist who'd never made good of anything in his life. And this brilliant piece of modern literature, 'How to have everything you ever wanted', by Sir Archibald Smythe-Flannigan. A self proclaimed millionaire whose advice is sought by great leaders from around the globe. The truth is, the man is a compulsive liar and there not being a shred of evidence to back up any of his claims. He uses a pseudonym so he can't be traced in Who's Who or Google. In reality he's an old lag currently doing 15 years for swindling funds from orphanages. Now do you see?'

Drained of any will to resist further, 'I suppose I must accede to your professional integrity – will you advise me?'

'That's better. We'll call you. . . Zeus Maximus, infamous author of the dark arts. Don't worry, we can seed the internet with the name and various untraceable rumours. Father?'

'Er what do you mean, 'father'?

'Your father dopey, who was he?'

'He was a simple cobbler, his mum died young, and he fought in the Second World War. That's it really, no one special. . . Oh, he did guard Balmoral Castle once when he was in an Anti Aircraft company of the Artillery.'

'Mmm, okay – let's see, brilliant author inherits wisdom of his father, his whole life coloured by the presence of an unsung war hero. Zeus' father, who we cannot name for legal reasons, was born into poverty and orphaned along with his siblings at an early age. Sent to work aged fourteen, five years later he was first in line to volunteer to serve king and country against the fascist hordes that were sweeping Europe. He was selected for secondment to a crack Anti Aircraft unit to protect royalty at Balmoral Castle. It was later rumoured that the aristocratic elite had fraternised liberally with young soldiers. This may explain why so many were transferred to other regiments and sent in on D Day, conceivably to purge witnesses to the infamous 'Balmoral affair'. Changing his name again on return to Blighty he became a successful and self-made leather goods industrialist. He never spoke openly of his loves and trials in life but in this enlightening book, Zeus Maximus reveals all he knows and more, shedding long awaited light on the eccentric social past of Great Britain. That'll do for a start –Mavis will knock it about a bit – should make a best seller – we can easily buy a few prestigious awards for it and enter it into our own competitions where we can guarantee you coming first. Nothing to it really, if you just have the will to face the truth.'

M. F. de C. 2016

There comes a time, when all bonds are slipped and one drifts free of the other.
Commonality, confined to history alone.

40

Emily's Friend.

One misty September morning, 1894, it was just after seven in the little moor side cottage. 'If she's not ready soon, I won't be taking her to the mill with me,' George said to his wife, Victoria.

She smiled back and pointed to a small window that overlooked a narrow lane and the river beyond. 'Look there George, she's been waiting for you this last half hour. You know how she loves to visit the mill.'

George returned the smile, picked up the neatly packed lunch basket and replied, 'I know, I know. She's found a friend near the mill to play with.'

George reminded his wife that they might not be back till late, perhaps even after dark... but, 'everything would be fine.'

A cart hitched to two heavy horses stood in the lane ready to go. Shires they were, powerful, dependable and hard working creatures. George and daughter Emily, aged eight, climbed aboard and set off with a cheery wave. Soon they began the long climb that would take them through the wooded valley and on to the desolate moors.

The colours were already changing with the season and the autumn Sun shone warm and bright. The horses plodded steadily onwards, simply taking the moorland track in their stride. All was peaceful and happy. George whispered to Emily, 'Did you know, something is watching us from the hill to our left?' Emily peered at the hill, seeing nothing but bracken and gorse, then that something moved and she saw it immediately.

'Oh, isn't he wonderful? He must be the finest stag on the entire moor.' As the cart trundled on, Emily watched longingly as the great stag slowly faded into the distance. The great stag watched them go.

'Makes you wonder what else could be out there on the moor, just watching us as we go by, us not seeing, never even knowing,' said George, thoughtfully.

It made Emily think too and she edged closer on the wooden seat to her father's side.

As they neared their destination, the landscape began to change once more to wooded valleys. The mill was down at the very bottom of the valley and driven by water power from the small but fast flowing River Erle.

'Remember to keep away from the water, Emily. You must be . . .' George was interrupted before he could finish.

'Yes dad, I know. Be careful, stay away from the water and the machinery. I've been told a hundred times already,' said Emily with a hint of annoyance. 'My friend always warns me not to go any where near it.'

'Sensible friend that,' George thought, 'Emily seems to be well aware of the danger; I'll not mention it again.'

George drove the horses just past the mill building to a horse trough under a great beech tree where they were glad of the shade and cool drink.

'Come on Emily, let's go in and see the miller, then you can find your friend and play, while I help in the mill.' So saying, George lifted Emily down from the cart. They walked away hand in hand, leaving the sound of horses drinking and the shaking of heads and harness behind them.

'Perhaps I'll meet your friend this time Emily?' George asked.

'She'll probably turn up when all the old people are inside,' Emily replied with a touch of authority.

Emily and George entered the old stone building, where they were warmly greeted by the owner, a kindly man called Harry Baker, 'Welcome, George, good to see you again. . . and you too young Emily, how quickly you are growing up.'

'Right, Emily,' said George, 'we have business to attend to. Take the feed bag off the cart and give it to the horses, watch they don't stamp on your feet. Then you can play a while until call for you.'

The miller called after her, 'You keep away from the water young lady. You keep well away.' He sounded really stern. Not like him at all.

An hour or so later everything was ready for loading. George leaned his head out of the doorway to see where Emily had gone. She was sitting by a pile of logs talking to herself and giggling. He smiled to see his daughter playing so happily on her own. Obviously her friend hadn't turned up that day. It was a shame.

'Come along now, Emily. We must be off home. We want to be off the moors long before sunset.'

As they prepared to leave, Harry Baker the kindly miller pressed a shiny new copper penny into Emily's hand, 'spend it wisely my dear.'

Emily thanked him and with a smile, stepped outside, looking down at her new treasure. 'Lovely girl, your daughter George, reminds me so much of my own.

As they crossed the moorland track, George spoke with Emily about her friend who hadn't turned up that day.

'But she was there dad, Lizzie is always there, I suppose you just didn't see her,' Emily explained. 'Lizzie is a really happy girl, we're the same age and she's the miller's daughter. We always play by the logs and keep well away from the water, which she doesn't like at all.'

George wasn't sure what to believe; perhaps it was just childish imagination. 'Children are like that,' George thought, as he peered about the surrounding moor, wondering what else was out there that he couldn't see but could still see him.

As the afternoon wore on, the air cooled and the mist began to return, Emily sat closer still to her father, he gently flicked the reins and it wasn't long before they were off the moor. Great hooves clip clopped their way along the lane and the crunch of stones beneath the heavy iron rims of the cart wheels brought Victoria to the door to greet them with a smile. They were safely home before the darkness came and with much news to tell.

Back at the mill, work was finishing for the day. Dusk was fast approaching and the miller struck a match to light a lantern. He stopped by the doorway and brushed dust from a stone set in the wall. He smiled quietly with fond memories as he read the name in neatly carved letters,

"IN LOVING MEMORY OF LIZZIE BAKER. . ."

He brushed more dust away with his sleeve and now with a tear in his eye, read on.

". . . AGE EIGHT YEARS TWO MONTHS, DROWNED NEAR THIS PLACE,
FOURTH SEPTEMBER 1888."

'So often the real truth is hidden by what we prefer to think.'

41

The Phoebe-Marie
August 1878.
Genny's Cove, a village on England's Atlantic coast.

Sea birds were ominous by their silence and like the lone man in seafaring clothes at the end of the quay spellbound by the changing sky. A weathered hand touched his shoulder and disturbed his dreaming. Turning slowly, he shared a knowing smile and a greeting with William, his lifelong friend. The wind off the sea grew colder by the hour; no boats would set out that day.

Walking back along the quayside towards the fishing fleet resting at low tide they met others near the harbour steps, all eyes fixed towards the horizon. Andrew and William turned to look. A gust of wind flapped their collars, voices fading as the wind howled in their ears. There, far out to sea on a northerly tack, were sails.

For a while, a squall hid the ship from view. 'She's closer inshore already Andrew, I can't say I like the look of that; no, not at all,' William's voice, uneasy.

Andrew nodded thoughtfully, this was a coastline he knew well, from hard won experience.

Together they watched a while longer, until a new bitterness in the wind and the threat of heavy rain drove them to seek shelter.

Aboard the ketch, *Auckland*, Captain Sam Harvey faced a dilemma. On board was the ship's elderly owner, John Lightfoot Esq., and his family. Intended to be a treat from the owner for his grandchildren, all were now sick with sea and fear. None had expected such terrifying weather. Had he not been ordered otherwise by the owner, a rich and powerful man, though ignorant of the sea, the captain would have sailed far from shore and waited out the storm. His only other choice was to find anchorage in a sheltered bay along the coast, yet on this rocky sea shore safe harbours were few. Studying the charts he found a bay whose southern edge would give shelter. Influenced by a dictatorial owner, the Captain gave orders to sail for Yenisbury Bay. A bay with no safe beach, their anchor must hold. A reluctant crew set to, making way for the line of white water which separates sea from cliff. Once past the point of no return, the bay became their abiding hope but the wind strengthened and drove them shoreward towards a coastline never shy of death.

At Genny's Cove, Andrew chopped logs at his cottage, readying the winter's wood supply, his wife Elizabeth preparing food in the kitchen. When the roof tiles started to rattle, Andrew walked through the house picking up his coat on the way. Elizabeth said nothing for she knew where he was going. The same place he always went when the weather was bad. Cloth cap tight on his head, and collar up, he strode purposefully along the narrow village street, his fisherman's boots strangely quiet on the tanned stone cobbles. When Andrew arrived at the boat house he found the rear door already open. He approached slowly to stand in the doorway. He heard voices and stopped to listen.

'Large axe; check it's sharp. Hatchets, two, and sharp, throwing lines, under the seats, three spare oars and the anchor. . 'At that point William spotted Andrew in the doorway, 'I knew you'd be down here Andrew.'

First, acknowledging his friend with a raised hand, 'You helping your uncle William out then David? You'll not go wrong listening to him.'

An hour later, heavy hoof beats of a farm horse clattered on the cobbles outside. 'Thank God you're already here. You've heard the news then?' The farmer was breathless, but they understood well enough. 'I was fetching sheep off the south foreland by Yenisbury Bay, there's a ship in trouble. One mast looks broken to me and she's close by the rocks already. . . I saw people on deck. . . '

A change of mood swept away all pleasantries.

'William. Put up a maroon and raise a crew, David, open the front doors then help with the launch,' and seeing the eager look on David's face, added, 'but you'll not be coming with us.'

Andrew turned to prepare for action and spread open the sea chart, his mind racing. A heart stopping boom shook the village. It wasn't long before volunteers filled the boathouse. With wind and tide running the way it was, this voyage would test the strongest crew. Andrew, their trusted coxswain, walked among them picking a dozen men with a firm hand to each chosen shoulder. As horses and ropes were prepared for the launch, Andrew gathered the chosen ones about the sea chart, 'Dismasted vessel in Yenisbury Bay,' Andrew paused, while a murmur of dismay came from his crew. 'She's already on, or close to the rocks, tide is on the flood and the wind unfavourable to say the least. Her crew has been seen on deck.'

On board the half wrecked ketch in Yenisbury Bay, the sailors sensed their fate. They were realistic about any chance of survival as the pounding sea met jagged rocks. Death might reach out its unwelcome hand and touch them at any minute and the creaking of ship's timbers and flapping of tattered sails had long driven terror into the poor children's hearts.

Phoebe-Marie's crew and helpers rallied their strength and launched into a sea of wild white horses driven ashore under an ever menacing sky. Andrew had picked his strongest crew well and as he called upon them to pull together he steered them beyond the worst of the inshore waves.

On board the ketch a watery grave might beckon but Captain Sam Harvey continued to reassure his passengers that all would be well. He could only hope that their end would come quick and clean, though a desperate yearning for salvation would haunt them all to the very end. If the ketch survived intact, she might be stranded by the outgoing tide. Then they might all walk along the shore line to safety. But, such a hope was like the drowning man clinging to straws. The *Auckland* looked unlikely to last until the tide had ebbed.

As for our valiant lifeboat, now some distance from shore, many a time wind and wave contrived to capsize her as the storm met her beam on. Yet the skill of the coxswain and the strength of her crew prevailed again and again. It was more than two miles to Yenisbury Bay with the storm pushing them ever closer to the sea cliffs that rise a thousand feet or more. 'Set the for'ard sail, we'll take advantage of this wind where we can. Two men raised the mast and set the sail, an astonishing feat as the small boat was buffeted mercilessly by the elements. Spray stung their hands and faces; their clothes were soaked in sweat. Water swilled about their feet as the self balers struggled to keep up.

'There she is! I see her, off the starboard quarter. Take courage lads and save something for the journey home,' Andrew shouted, steering with one hand and pointing with another.

As the lifeboat edged ever closer, Andrew made his plan.

The *Auckland* was indeed dis-masted, sails shredded and rigging a tangled mess in the foam. She was pinned to the rocks by the wind and the rising tide. However, Andrew could see a little slack water by her bows. 'That's where we'll take them off,' he thought, then called for the sail to be lowered and mast stowed.

'Put up a flare Jack, let them know we are here.' With all the skill of a master mariner, Andrew picked his spot to turn, anchor and line up, drifting *Phoebe-Marie* stern first towards the ketch.

From the stern rail of the *Auckland*, Captain Harvey and his first mate watched through spray stung eyes as the lifeboat crew reduced oars and paid out the anchor line. It seemed to take forever, as though time itself had stopped to watch such a spectacle.

Once at anchor and no longer making way, the *Phoebe-Marie* pitched and rolled with every wave. Andrew pointed to the bows of the *Auckland* with outstretched arm.

As of one mind, Captain and mate made their way forward, gathering the crew as they went. Captain Harvey shouted into the cabin, 'Be of good cheer sir, we may still be saved. . . lifeboat coming. Stay below, not safe yet.'

As the *Phoebe-Marie* slowly came alongside, Andrew organised his rescue party, some used oars to keep her from striking the hull, and others prepared the throwing lines. 'Prepare to take a line on board,' Andrew hollered above the noise of sea on rocks, and then more quietly to his crew, 'standby to cut lines if need be, we've got this far, we'll not be dragged down with her if she sinks.'

Captain Harvey's crew set about with renewed vigour to secure the throwing line and despite numbed hands, the knots were tied with skill, 'All secure Cap'n, all secure.' Captain Harvey immediately ordered a rope ladder over the side.

Andrew determined to board the *Auckland* and assess the situation for himself. On a rising wave he reached out for the rope ladder and began to climb, the wave nearly sweeping him out to sea. Helped over the ship's rail by eager hands Andrew was soon on deck. A handshake with the captain, an exchange of names and damage to *Auckland* was quickly assessed. Taking the captain to one side, 'We can take ten Sam,' he confided, 'and no promise we can make it back for the rest of you.'

Sam nodded solemnly, the nod of a man preparing for his own funeral. An honourable man, he knew he must stay with his ship, 'You choose then Andrew, for I cannot.'

Choosing was not so much a hardship for Andrew; he'd done it many a time before. Andrew surveyed the pleading eyes of the crew; no one wants to die, not like this. He chose six strong sailors who could help his own crew with rowing and the woman with her three terrified young children but the elderly gentleman looked like he'd seen most of his days already and his survival was questionable. 'Right Sam, put the chosen men on board the *Phoebe-Marie* then we'll help the woman and children aboard ourselves.

While the waves battered the creaking ketch steadily towards her inevitable surrender and hanging with one arm from the rope ladder, Andrew lowered the three children one by one to the waiting arms of his crew. Their mother was already weakened by her ordeal and as the lifeboat rose and fell, the frightened children watched in horror as she lost her grip on the swaying ladder. Andrew reached out and caught her with almost super human effort. She was helped aboard to sit centre of *Phoebe-Marie* with her children huddled around her. It wasn't without a price to pay, Andrew had felt something tear in his shoulder, and it wasn't his coat. He was in pain already as his crew pulled him strongly towards them and into relative safety. Certainly Andrew didn't want a fuss; his crew looked to him for leadership as well as seamanship. He would just have to steer with one arm, that's all.

From the rail of the ketch, the forsaken remnants of the crew watched as the life or death struggle played out before their eyes. When the *Phoebe-Marie* left the slack water by the *Auckland's* bows she met breaking waves that sought to beat her against the ship's hull. Suddenly, like gun shots, two oars were broken, their splintered remains quickly lost to the deep. Above the noise of the wind that drove white horses to their untimely death on the rocks, they could hear Andrew's commanding voice, 'heave, men, heave on that line. Oars together now. . . pull men, pull.'

Slowly but surely, the *Phoebe-Marie* made progress, anchor aboard, they were at last heading for home.

Andrew looked southwards towards Genny's Cove but all he saw was white water and spray. It seemed, row and die or stay and die, though such men gave up only when their hearts stopped beating.

Meeting the wind head on, the lifeboat crew pulled hard on the oars in silent unison, the mark of a disciplined crew. Adrenalin gradually drained from Andrew's body, replaced by pain in his damaged shoulder. Steeling himself, he braced his body against the tiller and set his eyes on a course for home. Against rising waves and blinding spindrift Andrew guided his gallant crew, reading the waves and seeking every advantage. The crew, with backs to a hungry sea, timed their stroke with the man in front and listened for their coxswain's orders.

They'd already lost sight of the *Auckland* and only home filled their thoughts. Blistered hands hauled away at heavy oars while death hunted them close by in the deep. When a man began to tire and a chance came, he changed him for one of the sailors he'd rescued. An unwarranted sense of guilt made the crew reluctant to give up their place, ashamed to meet the eyes of their comrades. Then, once at rest, sweat and sea water cooled quickly and brought a shiver to their bones. Little by little, the *Phoebe-Marie* and her precious cargo made progress against wind and tide. A remarkable feat of strength and courage, few would have thought possible.

Yet another half hour and Genny's Cove was just visible. Now was not the time to relax, now was the time to redouble efforts. Whatever the cost, there must be no mistakes.

'Land ho, off port quarter. . . home in sight,' Andrew cried. The news gave the crew renewed strength.

Genny's Cove lookouts had already seen the coloured speck appearing and disappearing in the distant waves. Willing villagers prepared to receive the boat into harbour and the boat house was ready with blankets, dry clothes and food.

Finally, *Phoebe-Marie* was rowed safely into the relative calm of the harbour to welcoming shouts from the villagers. Safe home and on dry land, the relief of the crew was immense. The deep indeed, had failed to claim them.

Fresh volunteers secured *Phoebe-Marie* to the quayside, while the rescued mother and her children were comforted in the boat house.

Andrew, however, was already planning the next mission. . . his clear orders calling for replacement oars and an additional anchor and line. As the exhausted crew dragged themselves off to the boathouse, fresh legged volunteers busied themselves with returning the lifeboat to sea readiness.

Andrew disguised his pain and also made his way to the boat-house. He sensed he was the only one who might make the repeat journey with any chance of success; lives depended on him and his leadership.

'Quiet please! It's not over,' Andrew shouted, bringing an instant hush to the gathered crowd. All eyes were on him. It seemed that hardly a breath was taken, 'we must go again, and soon, for she'll not take much more of this sea. Volunteers only, step forward, this will not be easy, make no mistake. None from the last trip, no one can row this sea twice. I'll take anyone who can pull a decent oar. Yes, you, you and you, get rigged for sea and wait by the boat. . . alright David, you can make up the numbers but you must row like the devil is after you, for he most certainly will be. . .'

David nodded with a sense of pride in his heart that he was now among the chosen, picked up a life vest and joined the others on the quayside. Andrew saw the worried look in William's eyes.

Perhaps Andrew was pinning his hopes on the weather abating and making life easier, for he'd picked his strongest crew for the first run and now look at them. . . keen in spirit but drained in body. Once again he called the crew to action as the lifeboat cleared the calm water and met the wild sea, 'Oars together now. . . pull men, pull.' Soon she was lost from sight in the spray, somewhere out there upon the deep.

Of those left ashore, some went to work or home to rest, others stayed at the boat house, those that did, cheered themselves with the success of an amazing rescue. While they eagerly awaited the lookout's cry that the *Phoebe-Marie* was homeward bound again, as of one mind, they talked of the strength of their fine boat and the men who served.

After two or more anxious hours, hoof beats of a farm horse clattered on the cobbles outside the boathouse. William stood and in silence, walked outside. . .

Now I must tell you, we have already stayed too long. It's time we left the villagers of Genny's Cove to their own fate, whatever that may be.

The village fades from our sight but our hearing lingers long enough and before it is gone forever, we hear the impatient stamp of horse shoes on cobbles and a familiar farmer's voice calling to William . . . 'I've something for you. . .' a gust of wind howls and it is difficult to hear clearly, then a lull and we hear William exclaim with great joy and a hint of curiosity, 'David! David my boy, it's you. How. . .?'

'Uncle, all is well, we saved them all. . . beached on next cove along, resting crew. . . skipper said he'd never hear the last of it if he didn't send me back to you with the news.'

On 12th September1878, young David Trescothick received the silver medal for gallantry. He never missed another shout and on Andrew's retirement took over the role of Coxswain. None were more proud than his uncle William. The lifeboat station was closed in 1926 but his medal remains on display in the small village museum.

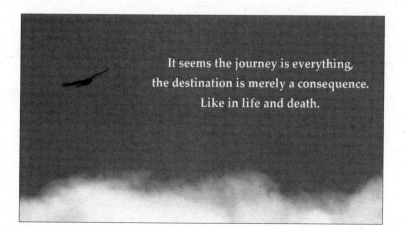

It seems the journey is everything,
the destination is merely a consequence.
Like in life and death.

Edward Gaskell
publishers
DEVON